The Letter, the Witch,
and the Ring

OTHER YEARLING BOOKS YOU WILL ENJOY:

YEARLING BOOKS are designed especially to entertain and enlighten young people. Charles F. Reasoner, Professor Emeritus of Children's Literature and Reading, New York University, is consultant to this series.

For a complete listing of all Yearling titles, write to Dell Publishing Co., Inc., Promotion Department, P.O. Box 3000, Pine Brook, N.J. 07058.

THE LETTER,
THE WITCH,
AND THE RING

JOHN BELLAIRS
drawings by Richard Egielski

A YEARLING BOOK

Published by
Dell Publishing Co., Inc.
1 Dag Hammarskjold Plaza
New York, New York 10017

Text copyright © 1976 by John Bellairs
Pictures copyright © 1976 by The Dial Press

Yearling ® TM 913705, Dell Publishing Co., Inc.

ISBN: 0-440-44722-4

Reprinted by arrangement with The Dial Press
Printed in the United States of America
Seventh Dell printing—September 1984

CW

For my son, Frank

The Letter, the Witch,
and the Ring

CHAPTER ONE

"No, no, no, NO! I will not wear that silly uniform!"
Rose Rita Pottinger stood in the middle of her bedroom
floor. She was in her underwear, and she was glaring
angrily at her mother, who held in her arms a freshly
ironed girl scout uniform.

"Well, then, what am I going to do with it?" Mrs.
Pottinger asked wearily.

"Throw it out!" Rose Rita screamed. She grabbed the
uniform from her mother and flung it to the floor. Tears
were in Rose Rita's eyes now. Her face felt hot and
flushed. "Take it out and put it on a scarecrow or something! I tell you once and for all, Mother, I am *not*
going to be a girl scout or a campfire girl, I am *not* going

to Camp Kitch-itti-Kippi this summer and roast marsh-mallows and sing happy songs, I am going to spend this whole rotten summer batting a tennis ball against the side of the house until I'm so sick and . . . so sick and . . ." Rose Rita broke down. She put her hands over her face and cried.

Mrs. Pottinger put her arm around Rose Rita and helped her sit down on the bed. "There, there," she said, patting Rose Rita's shoulder. "It's not so bad as all that . . ."

Rose Rita flung her hands away from her face. She tore off her glasses and sat staring blearily at her mother. "Oh yes it is, Mom. It's every bit as bad as all that. It's awful! I wanted to spend the summer with Lewis and have a good time, and now he's going to that dumb boy scout camp. He'll be out there till school starts again, and I'm stuck here in this dumb town with nothing to do and nobody to have fun with."

Mrs. Pottinger sighed. "Well, maybe you can find another boy friend."

Rose Rita put her glasses back on and gave her mother a dirty look. "Mom, how many times do I have to tell you? Lewis isn't my boy friend, he's my *best* friend, just like Marie Gallagher used to be. I don't see why it should have to be any different just because he's a boy and I'm a girl."

Mrs. Pottinger smiled patiently at her daughter. "Well, my dear, it is different, and that's something you've got to understand. Lewis is twelve now, and you're thirteen. You and I are going to have to have a little talk on this subject."

Rose Rita turned away and watched a fly that was buzzing around on the window screen. "Oh, Mom, I don't want to have a little talk. Not now, anyway. I just want you to leave me alone."

Mrs. Pottinger shrugged her shoulders and got up. "Very well, Rose Rita. Whatever you want. By the way, what are you giving Lewis as a going-away present?"

"I bought him a genuine official Boy Scout Fire-Starting Kit," said Rose Rita sullenly. "And you know what? I hope he sets fire to himself with it and gets third-degree burns."

"Now, Rose Rita," said her mother soothingly. "You know very well that you don't want anything like that."

"I don't, huh? Well, let me tell you something, Mom . . ."

"I'll see you later, Rose Rita," said her mother, cutting her off. Mrs. Pottinger didn't want to listen to another of her daughter's ill-tempered outbursts. She was afraid that if she did, she might lose her temper herself.

Mrs. Pottinger got up and left the room, closing the door softly behind her. Rose Rita was alone. She threw herself down on the bed and cried. She cried for quite a while, but instead of feeling better after her cry, she felt worse. Rose Rita got up and glanced wildly around the room, searching for something that might cheer her up.

Maybe she could get out her bat and ball and go down to the athletic field and hit some flies. That usually made her feel good. She opened the door of her closet and immediately another wave of sadness swept over her. There, hanging forlornly on a nail, was her black beanie. She had worn it for years, but now it seemed silly to her. For half a year the black beanie had been hanging in the closet, gathering dust. Now, for some reason, the sight of it made Rose Rita burst into tears again.

What was wrong with her? Rose Rita would have given a lot to know. Maybe it had something to do with being thirteen. She was a teenager now, and not a kid. Next fall she would be in the seventh grade. Seventh and eighth grades were in Junior High. The junior high kids went to school in a big black stone building next to the high school. They had lockers in the halls like the high school kids, and they even had their own gym where they had Saturday night dances. But Rose Rita didn't want to go to dances. She didn't want to go on dates, with Lewis or anybody else. All she wanted was to keep on being a kid. She wanted to play baseball, and climb trees, and build ship models with Lewis. She looked forward to Junior High about as much as she looked forward to a visit to the dentist.

Rose Rita closed the closet door and turned away. As she turned, she happened to catch sight of herself in the mirror. She saw a tall skinny homely girl with black stringy hair and eyeglasses. I should have been a boy, Rose Rita thought. Homely boys didn't have as many problems as homely girls did. Also, boys could go to boy scout camp, and girls couldn't. Boys could get together for a game of flies and grounders and nobody thought there was anything strange about it. Boys didn't have to wear nylons and pleated skirts and starched blouses to church on Sunday. As fas as Rose Rita was concerned, boys really had the life. But she had been born a girl, and there didn't seem to be much she could do about it.

Rose Rita went over to the goldfish tank and fed her fish. She started to whistle and did a little dance around the room. Outside it was a beautiful day. The sun was shining. People were watering their lawns and kids were riding their bikes. Maybe if she didn't think about her problems, they would go away. It might turn out to be a nice summer after all.

That night Rose Rita went to Lewis's going-away-to-camp party. She didn't really want to go, but she figured she had to. Lewis was still her best friend, even though he was leaving her in the lurch by going away to camp, and she didn't want to hurt his feelings. Lewis lived in a big old house up on High Street. He lived with his uncle Jonathan, who was a wizard. And the lady next door, Mrs. Zimmermann, was a witch. Jonathan and Mrs. Zimmermann didn't run around in black robes waving wands, but they did know how to do magic.

Rose Rita figured that Mrs. Zimmermann knew more magic than Jonathan did, but she didn't show off so much.

The party that night turned out to be so much fun that Rose Rita forgot all about her troubles. She even forgot that she was supposed to be mad at Lewis. Mrs. Zimmermann taught Lewis and Rose Rita a couple of new card games (klaberjass and six-pack bezique, Winston Churchill's favorite card game), and Jonathan did one of his magic illusions, where he made everyone think that they were stumping across the floor of the Atlantic in diving suits. They visited some sunken galleons and the wreck of the *Titanic*, and even watched an octopus fight. Then the show was over, and it was time for lemonade and chocolate chip cookies. Everyone went out on the front porch and ate and drank and swung on the glider and laughed and talked until it was very late.

After the party was over, around midnight, Rose Rita was sitting in Mrs. Zimmermann's kitchen. She was staying over at Mrs. Zimmermann's house tonight, something that she always liked to do. Mrs. Zimmermann was really like a second mother to Rose Rita. Rose Rita felt that she could talk to her about practically anything. Now she was sitting there at the kitchen table, crumbling up the last chocolate chip cookie and watching Mrs. Zimmermann as she stood at the stove in her purple

summer nightgown. She was heating up some milk in a little pan. Mrs. Zimmermann always had to drink hot milk to calm down after parties. She hated the taste of the stuff, but it was the only way she could get to sleep.

"Some party, eh, Rosie?" she said, stirring the milk.

"Yeah. It sure was."

"You know," said Mrs. Zimmermann slowly, "I didn't even want there to be a party."

Rose Rita was startled. "You didn't?"

"Nope. I was afraid your feelings would be hurt. Even more than they already were, I mean—by Lewis's running out on you."

Rose Rita had not told Mrs. Zimmermann how she felt about Lewis's going away. She was amazed at how much Mrs. Zimmermann understood about her. Maybe it all went with being a witch.

Mrs. Zimmermann tested the milk with her finger. Then she poured it into a mug that was decorated with little purple flowers. She sat down across from Rose Rita and took a sip.

"Ugh!" said Mrs. Zimmermann, making a face. "I think the next time I'll slip myself a mickey. But back to what we were talking about. You're pretty mad at Lewis, aren't you?"

Rose Rita stared at the table. "Yeah, I sure am. If I hadn't liked you and Uncle Jonathan so much, I don't think I'd've showed up at all."

Mrs. Zimmermann chuckled. "It didn't look as if you

and he were on the best of terms tonight. Do you have any idea of why he's going to camp?"

Rose Rita crumbled up her cookie and thought. "Well," she said at last, "I guess he's tired of palling around with me and so he wants to be a big eagle scout or something."

"You're about half right," said Mrs. Zimmermann. "That is, he does want to be a boy scout. But he isn't tired of being your friend. I think Lewis wishes very much that you could be going to camp with him."

Rose Rita blinked back her tears. "He does?"

Mrs. Zimmermann nodded. "Yes, and I'll tell you something else. He can't wait to get back and tell you about all the great new things he's learned to do."

Rose Rita looked confused. "I don't understand. It sounds all mixed up. He likes me so he's going away so he can tell me how much fun it was not to have me around."

Mrs. Zimmermann laughed. "Well, when you put it that way, my dear, it does sound mixed up. And I will admit that it's all mixed up in Lewis's head. He wants to learn how to tie knots and paddle canoes and hike through the wilderness, and he wants to come back and tell you so you'll think he's a real boy and like him even more than you do now."

"I like him just the way he is. What's all this dumb stuff about being a real boy?"

Mrs. Zimmermann sat back and sighed. There was a

long silver case lying on the table. She picked it up and opened it. Inside was a row of dark brown cigars.

"Do you mind if I smoke?"

"Nope." Rose Rita had seen Mrs. Zimmermann smoking cigars before. It had surprised her at first, but she had gotten used to it. As she watched, Mrs. Zimmermann bit the end off the cigar and spat it into a nearby wastebasket. Then she snapped her fingers and a match appeared out of thin air. When the cigar was lit, Mrs. Zimmermann offered the match back to the air, and it disappeared.

"Saves on ashtrays," she said, grinning. Mrs. Zimmermann took a few puffs. The smoke trailed off toward the open window in long graceful swirls. There was a silence. Finally Mrs. Zimmermann spoke again. "I know it's hard for you to understand, Rose Rita. It's always hard to understand why someone is doing something that hurts us. But think of what Lewis is like; he's a pudgy shy boy who's always got his nose stuck in a book. He isn't good at sports, and he's scared of practically everything. Well. Then look at you. You're a regular tomboy. You can climb trees, you can run fast, and the other day when I was watching you, you struck out the side in that girls' softball game. You can do all the things that Lewis can't do. Now do you see why he's going to camp?"

Rose Rita couldn't believe what she was thinking. "To be like me?"

Mrs. Zimmermann nodded. "Exactly. To be like you,

so you'll like him better. Of course, there are other reasons. For instance, he'd like to be like other boys. He wants to be normal—most bright kids do." She smiled wryly and flicked cigar ashes into the sink.

Rose Rita looked sad. "If he'd've asked me, I would've taught him a lot of stuff."

"No good. He can't learn from a girl—it would hurt his pride. But look, all this talk is beside the point. Lewis is going off to camp tomorrow, and you're stuck here in New Zebedee with nothing to do. Well now, it just so happens that the other day I received a most surprising letter. It was from my late cousin Oley. Have I ever mentioned him to you?"

Rose Rita thought a second. "Gee, no, I don't think so."

"I didn't think I had. Well, Oley was a strange old duck, but . . ."

Rose Rita cut in. "Mrs. Zimmermann, you said 'late.' Is he . . ."

Mrs. Zimmermann nodded sadly. "Yes, I'm afraid Oley has gone to glory. He wrote me a letter while he was dying, and . . . well, see here now, why don't I just go get it and show it to you? It'll give you some idea of the kind of person he was."

Mrs. Zimmermann got up and went upstairs. For a while Rose Rita heard her banging around and shuffling papers in her large untidy study. When she came downstairs, she handed Rose Rita a wrinkled piece of paper with several little holes punched in it. There was writing on the paper, but it was very sloppy and shaky. Ink had been spilled in several places.

"This letter came with a bunch of legal documents for me to sign," said Mrs. Zimmermann. "It's all a very odd business and I'm not sure I know what to think of it. Anyhow, there's the letter. It's a mess, but you can read it. Oh, by the way, Oley always wrote with a quill pen when he felt he had something important to say. That's what made all those holes in the paper. Go ahead. Read it."

Rose Rita picked up the letter. It said:

May 21, 1950

Dear Florence,

This may well be the last letter I ever write. I fell ill suddenly last week, and do not understand it, since I have never had a sick day in my life until now. I don't believe in doctors, as you know, and have been trying to cure myself. I bought some medicine at the store down the road, but it hasn't helped a bit. So, as they say, it looks as if I am on my way out. In fact, when you get this letter, I will be dead, since I have left instructions for it to be sent to you with my will in case I kick off, as they say.

Now then, on to business. I am leaving you my farm. You are my only living relative, and I've always liked you, though I know you haven't cared

that much for me. Anyway, let's let bygones be by-
gones. The farm is yours, and I hope you enjoy it.
And here is one final very important note. You
remember the Battle Meadow? Well, I was digging
there the other day, and I came across a magic
ring. I know you will think I'm kidding, but when
you handle the thing and try it on, you will know
I was right. I haven't told anyone about the ring,
except for a neighbor down the road. Maybe I am
a little funny in the head, but I know what I know,
and I think the ring is magic. I have locked the
ring in the lower left-hand drawer of my desk, and
I am going to have my lawyer send the key to you,
along with the key to the front door of the house.
So I guess that is all I have to say for now. With
luck I'll see you again some day, and if not, well,
I'll see you in the funny papers as they say, ha, ha.

> *Your cousin,*
> *Oley Gunderson*

"Wow!" said Rose Rita, as she handed the letter back to Mrs. Zimmermann. "What a weird letter!"

"Yes," said Mrs. Zimmermann, shaking her head sadly, "it's a weird letter from a rather weird person. Poor Oley! He lived all his life up there on that farm. Completely alone. No family, no friends, no neighbors, no nothing. I think it must have affected his mind."

Rose Rita's face fell. "You mean . . ."

Mrs. Zimmermann sighed. "Yes, my dear. I'm sorry to

disappoint you about that magic ring, but Oley was right when he said he was a little funny in the head. I think he made things up to make his life more interesting. That part about the Battle Meadow is right out of his childhood. A little bit of make-believe that he saved up. The trouble is, he saved it so long that he got to believing it was true."

"I don't get what you mean," said Rose Rita.

"It's all very simple. You see, when I was a girl, I used to go up to Oley's farm a lot. His dad Sven was alive then. He was a very generous sort, and was always inviting cousins and aunts up to stay for long periods of time. Oley and I used to play together, and one summer we found some Indian arrowheads in a meadow by a stream that runs out behind this farmhouse. Well, you know how kids are. On the basis of this little discovery we made up a story about how this had been a place where a battle had been fought between some settlers and a band of Indians. We even gave names to some of the Indians and pioneers who were involved in the battle, and we named the little field where we played the Battle Meadow. I had forgotten all about the Battle Meadow until Oley sent me this letter."

Rose Rita felt very disappointed. "Are you sure the part about the ring isn't true? I mean, sometimes even crazy people tell the truth. They really do, you know."

Mrs. Zimmermann smiled sympathetically at Rose Rita. "I'm sorry, my dear, but I'm afraid I know more about Oley Gunderson than you do. He was completely batty. Batty as a bedbug. But, batty or not, he left me his farm, and there are no other relatives around to contest the will on the grounds of insanity. So I'm going up there to have a look at the farm and sign a few papers. The farm is near Petoskey, right up at the tip of the Lower Peninsula, so after I've taken care of the legal folderol, I'm going to take the ferry across to the Upper Peninsula and drive all over the place. I haven't been on a really long car trip since gas rationing ended, and I've just bought a new car. I'm itching to go. Would you like to go with me?"

Rose Rita was overjoyed. She felt like jumping across the table and hugging Mrs. Zimmermann. But then a disturbing thought came to her. "Do you think my folks'd let me go?"

Mrs. Zimmermann smiled her most businesslike and competent smile. "It's all arranged. I called up your mother a couple of days ago to see if it would be all right with her. She said it sounded like a fine idea. We decided to save the news for you as a surprise."

There were tears in Rose Rita's eyes now. "Gee, Mrs. Zimmermann, thanks a lot. Thanks a whole lot."

"Don't mention it, my dear." Mrs. Zimmermann glanced at the kitchen clock. "I think we'd better be getting off to bed if we're going to be in any shape for tomorrow. Jonathan and Lewis will be coming over here for breakfast. Then off goes Lewis to camp, and off goes we to the wilds of Michigan." Mrs. Zimmermann got up and stubbed out her cigar in the kitchen sink. She went into the front room and started turning out lights. When she returned to the kitchen, she found Rose Rita still sitting at the table with her head in her hands. There was a dreamy look on her face.

"Still mooning about magic rings, eh?" said Mrs. Zimmermann. She laughed softly and patted Rose Rita on the back. "Rose Rita, Rose Rita," she said, shaking her head, "the trouble with you is, you've been hanging around with a witch, and you think magic is going to sprout up out of the cracks in the sidewalk, like dandelions. By the way, did I tell you? I don't have a magic umbrella anymore."

Rose Rita turned and stared at Mrs. Zimmermann in disbelief. "You *don't?*"

"Nope. As you recall, my old one got smashed in a battle with an evil spirit. It's totally done for. As for the new one, the one Jonathan bought me for Christmas, I haven't been able to do anything with it. I'm still a witch, of course. I can still snap matches out of the air. But as for the more serious, more powerful kinds of magic . . . well, I'm afraid I'm back in the bush leagues. I can't do anything."

Rose Rita felt awful. She had seen Mrs. Zimmermann's magic umbrella in action. Most of the time it just looked like a ratty old black umbrella, but when Mrs. Zimmermann said certain words to it, it turned into a tall rod topped by a crystal sphere, a sphere with a purple star burning inside it. It was the source of all Mrs. Zimmermann's greater powers. And now it was gone. Gone for good.

"Isn't . . . isn't there anything you can do, Mrs. Zimmermann?" Rose Rita asked.

" 'Fraid not, my dear. I'm just a parlor magician like Jonathan now, and I'll have to make the best of it. Sorry. Now, run up to bed. We've got a long day of traveling ahead of us."

Sleepily Rose Rita climbed the stairs. She was staying in the guest room. It was a very pleasant room, and, like most of the rooms in Mrs. Zimmermann's house, it was full of purple things. The wallpaper was covered with little bouquets of violets, and the chamber pot in the corner was made of purple Crown Derby china. Over the bureau hung a painting of a room in which almost everything was purple. The painting was signed "H. Matisse." It had been given to Mrs. Zimmermann by the famous French painter during her visit to Paris just before the First World War.

Rose Rita lay back on her pillow. The moon hung over Jonathan's house and cast a silver light on turrets and gables and steep slanted roofs. Rose Rita felt dreamy and strange. Magic umbrellas and magic rings were chasing each other around in her head. She thought about Oley's letter. What if there really was a magic ring up there, locked in his desk? That would sure be exciting. Rose Rita sighed and turned over on her side. Mrs. Zimmermann was a smart person. She usually knew what she was talking about, and she was probably right about that old ring. The whole story was just a lot of baloney. But as she drifted off to sleep, Rose Rita couldn't help thinking how nice it would be if Oley's letter were telling the truth.

CHAPTER TWO

Next morning Mrs. Zimmermann made popovers for breakfast. Just as she was pulling the pan out of the oven, the back door opened, and in walked Jonathan and Lewis. Lewis was pudgy and round-faced. He was wearing his brand-new boy scout uniform and a bright red neckerchief with BSA on the back. His hair was neatly parted and plastered down with Wildroot Cream Oil. Behind him came Jonathan. Jonathan always looked the same, summer or winter: red beard, pipe in mouth, tan wash pants, blue work shirt, red vest.

"Hi, Pruny!" said Jonathan, cheerfully. "Are those popovers ready yet?"

"The first batch is, Weird Beard," snapped Mrs. Zimmermann, as she dumped the heavy iron pan on the table. "I'm only making two pans. Think you can hold yourself down to four?"

"I'll be lucky if I get one, the way you grab them, Haggy. Watch out for her fork, Lewis. She stabbed me right here in the back of the hand last week."

Jonathan and Mrs. Zimmermann went on trading insults until breakfast was ready. Then, together with Lewis and Rose Rita, they sat down to the silent business of eating. At first Lewis didn't dare meet Rose Rita's eyes—he still felt bad about leaving her in the lurch. But then he noticed that she had a very smug look on her face. Jonathan noticed it too.

"Oh, all right!" said Jonathan, when he felt that he couldn't stand the suspense any longer. "What's the big secret? Rose Rita's got canary feathers all over her face."

"Oh, nothing much," said Rose Rita, grinning. "I'm just going up to explore around an old abandoned farm with Mrs. Zimmermann. The farm is supposed to be haunted, and there's a magic ring hidden somewhere in the house. It was put there by a madman who hanged himself later in the barn."

Lewis and Jonathan gaped. Rose Rita was embroidering a bit on the truth. It was one of her faults. Usually she was quite truthful, but when the occasion seemed to call for it, she could come out with the most amazing stuff.

Mrs. Zimmermann gave Rose Rita a sour look. "You ought to write books," she said dryly. Then she turned to Lewis and Jonathan. "Despite what my friend here claims, I am not running a Halloween Tourist Agency. My cousin Oley—you remember him, Jonathan—he died, and he left me his farm. I'm going up to see the place and drive around a bit, and I've asked Rose Rita to come with me. I'm sorry I didn't tell you about this before, Jonathan, but I was afraid you'd slip and spill the beans to Lewis. You know how good you are at keeping secrets."

Jonathan made a face at Mrs. Zimmermann, but she ignored him. "Well!" she said, sitting back and smiling broadly at Rose Rita and Lewis. "Now you both have something to do this summer, and that's how it should be!"

"Yeah," said Lewis sullenly. He was beginning to wonder if maybe Rose Rita wasn't getting the better deal after all.

After breakfast Lewis and Rose Rita volunteered to do the dishes. Mrs. Zimmermann went up to her study and brought down Oley's letter for Jonathan to see. He read it pensively while Rose Rita washed and Lewis wiped. Mrs. Zimmermann sat at the kitchen table, humming and smoking a cigar. When he had finished the letter, Jonathan handed it back to Mrs. Zimmermann without saying anything. He seemed thoughtful, though.

A few minutes later Jonathan got up and went next door to his house. He backed his big black car out of the driveway and pulled it up next to the curb. The back seat was full of Lewis's boy scout stuff: bed roll, pack, scout manual, hiking shoes, and a Quaker Oats box full of Mrs. Zimmermann's specialty—chocolate chip cookies.

Rose Rita and Mrs. Zimmermann stood at the curb. Jonathan was behind the wheel, and Lewis sat next to him.

"Well, good-by and *bon voyage*, and all that," said Mrs. Zimmermann. "Have a good time at camp, Lewis."

"Thanks, Mrs. Zimmermann," said Lewis, waving back.

"You two have a good time too, up there in the wilds of Michigan," said Jonathan. "Oh, by the way, Florence."

"Yes? What is it?"

"Just this: I think you ought to check out Oley's desk to see if there really is anything hidden away there. You never can tell."

Mrs. Zimmermann laughed. "If I find a magic ring, I'll send it to you by parcel post. But if I were you, I wouldn't hold my breath till it arrived. You've met Oley, Jonathan. You know how screwy he was."

Jonathan took his pipe out of his mouth and stared straight at Mrs. Zimmermann. "Yes, I know all about Oley, but just the same, I think you ought to watch out."

"Oh, sure, I'll watch out," said Mrs. Zimmermann carelessly. She really didn't feel that there was anything to worry about.

There were more good-bys and waves, and then Jonathan drove off. Mrs. Zimmermann told Rose Rita to run home and pack while she went inside to get her own things together.

Rose Rita ran off down the hill to her house. She was really excited by now, and impatient to get started. But just as she was opening the front door of her house, she heard her father say, "Well, I wish next time you'd consult me before you let our daughter go gallivanting off with the town screwball. For God's sake, Louise, don't you have any—"

Mrs. Pottinger cut him off. "Mrs. Zimmermann is not the town screwball," she said firmly. "She's a responsible person who's been a good friend to Rose Rita."

"Responsible, ha! She smokes cigars and she hobnobs around with old what's-his-name, the bearded character with all the money. The one who does magic tricks, you know his name . . ."

"Yes, I certainly do. And I would think that after your daughter had been the best friend of old what's-his-name's nephew for a solid year, the least you could do would be to learn his name. But I still can't see why . . ."

And on it went. Mr. and Mrs. Pottinger were arguing out in the kitchen, behind a closed door. But Mr. Pottinger had a loud voice, even when he was talking normally, and Mrs. Pottinger had raised her voice to match his. Rose Rita stood there a moment, listening. She knew from past experience that it would not be good to butt in on the argument. So she tiptoed quietly upstairs and started to pack.

Into the worn black valise that she used as a traveling bag Rose Rita threw underwear, shirts, jeans, toothbrush, toothpaste, and anything else she thought she would need. It felt great not to have to pack dresses and blouses and skirts. Mrs. Zimmermann never made Rose Rita get all dressed up—she let her wear what she liked. Rose Rita felt a sudden sense of hopelessness when she remembered that she wouldn't be able to be a tomboy forever. Skirts and nylons, lipsticks and powder puffs, dating and dancing were all waiting for her in Junior High. Wouldn't it be nice if she were really a boy? Then she could . . .

Rose Rita heard a horn beeping outside. That had to be Mrs. Zimmermann. She zipped up the valise and dashed downstairs with it. When she stepped out the front door, she found her mother standing there smiling. Her father was gone, so apparently the storm had blown over. Out at the curb was Mrs. Zimmermann. She was at the wheel of a brand-new 1950 Plymouth. It was high and boxy, and had a humpy sort of trunk. A strip of chrome divided the windshield in two, and the little square letters on the side of the car said CRANBROOK—

that was the name of that particular model. The car was bright green. Mrs. Zimmermann was angry about that, because she had ordered maroon, but she had been too lazy to send the car back.

"Hi, Rose Rita! Hi, Louise!" Mrs. Zimmermann called, waving to both of them. "Good day for traveling, eh?"

"I should say," said Mrs. Pottinger, smiling. She was genuinely happy that Rose Rita could be going on a trip with Mrs. Zimmermann. Mr. Pottinger's job kept the family in New Zebedee all through the summer, and Mrs. Pottinger had some idea of how lonely her daughter was going to be without Lewis. Fortunately Mrs. Pottinger did not know anything about Mrs. Zimmermann's magical abilities, and she distrusted the rumors she heard.

Rose Rita kissed her mother on the cheek. " 'Bye, Mom," she said. "See you in a couple of weeks."

"Okay. Have a good time," said Mrs. Pottinger. "Drop me a card when you get to Petoskey."

"I will."

Rose Rita ran down the steps, threw her valise in the back seat, and ran around to climb into the front seat beside Mrs. Zimmermann. Mrs. Zimmermann put the car in gear and they rolled off down Mansion Street. The trip had started.

Mrs. Zimmermann and Rose Rita took U.S. 12 over to U.S. 131, which runs straight north through Grand

Rapids. It was a beautiful sunny day. Telephone poles and trees and Burma-Shave signs whipped past. In the fields farm machines were working, machines with names like John Deere and Minneapolis-Moline and International Harvester. They were painted bright colors, blue and green and red and yellow. Every now and then Mrs. Zimmermann had to pull off onto the shoulder to let a tractor with a long cutting bar go by.

When they got to Big Rapids, Mrs. Zimmermann and Rose Rita had lunch in a diner. There was a pinball machine in the corner, and Mrs. Zimmermann insisted on playing it. Mrs. Zimmermann was a first-rate pinball player. She knew how to work the flippers, and—after she had been playing a particular machine for a while—she knew how much she could bang on the sides and the top without making the TILT sign light up. By the time she was through she had won thirty-five free games. She left them to be played off by the patrons of the diner, who were watching, open-mouthed. They had never seen a lady play a pinball machine before.

After lunch Mrs. Zimmermann went to the A&P and a bakery. She was planning to have a picnic supper at the farmhouse when they got there. Into the big metal cooler in the trunk she put salami, bologna, cans of deviled ham, a quart of vanilla ice cream, a bottle of milk, three bottles of pop, and a jar of pickles. Into a wooden picnic hamper she put two fresh loaves of salt-rising bread and a chocolate cake. She bought some crushed ice at a gas station and put it in the cooler to keep the food from spoiling. It was a hot day. The thermometer on the billboard that they passed on the way out of town said ninety.

Mrs. Zimmermann told Rose Rita that they were going to drive straight up to the farm now, without stopping. As they got farther and farther north, the hills began to grow steeper. Some of them looked as if the car would never be able to get up them, but it was funny how the hills seemed to flatten out under you as the car climbed. Now, all around her, Rose Rita saw pine trees. The wonderful fresh smell of them drifted in through the car windows as they sped along. They were approaching the vast forests of northern Michigan.

Late that afternoon Rose Rita and Mrs. Zimmermann were cruising slowly along a gravel road, listening to the weather report on the car radio. Without warning, the car began to slow down. It rolled to a halt. Mrs. Zimmermann turned the key and pumped the accelerator. All she got was the *rr-rr* sound of the starting motor trying to get the engine to turn over. But it wouldn't catch. After about the fifteenth try, Mrs. Zimmermann sat back and swore softly under her breath. Then she happened to glance at the gas gauge.

"Oh, don't *tell* me!" groaned Mrs. Zimmermann. She leaned forward and began hitting her forehead against the steering wheel.

"What's wrong?" asked Rose Rita.

Mrs. Zimmermann sat there with a disgusted expression on her face. "Oh, not much. We're just out of gas, that's all. I meant to fill up at that place where we bought the ice in Big Rapids, but I forgot."

Rose Rita put her hand to her mouth. "Oh no!"

"Oh yes. However, I know where we are. We're only a few miles from the farm. If you're feeling energetic, we could ditch the car and walk, but we don't even have to do that. There's a gas station a little ways up the road. At least, there used to be one."

Mrs. Zimmermann and Rose Rita got out of the car and started to walk. It was almost sunset. Clouds of midges hovered in the air, and the long shadows of trees lay across the road. Little patches of red light could be seen here and there among the roadside trees. Up and down hills the two travelers plodded, kicking up white dust as they went. Mrs. Zimmermann was a good walker, and so was Rose Rita. They reached the station just as the sun was going down.

Bigger's Grocery Store was surrounded on three sides by a dark forest of pines. The store was just a white frame house with a wide plate glass window in the front. Through the window you could see rows of stacked groceries and a cash register and counter in the rear. Some green letters on the window had once spelled SALADA, but now they just said ADA. Like many rural grocery stores, Bigger's was also a gas station. Out in front stood two red gas pumps, and near them was a white sign with a flying red horse on it. The horse was on the circular ornament on top of each pump too. In a weedy field next to the store stood a chicken coop. The coop stood in a fenced enclosure, but there were no chickens to be seen in the chicken yard. The tarpaper roof of the coop was caved in at one place, and the water pan in the yard had a thick green scum on it.

"Well, here we are," said Mrs. Zimmermann, wiping her forehead. "Now, if we can get Gert to come out and wait on us, we're all set."

Rose Rita was surprised. "Do you know the lady that runs this store?"

Mrs. Zimmermann sighed. "Yes, I'm afraid I do. I haven't been up this way for some time now, but Gert Bigger was running this store when I last came up to visit Oley. That was about five years ago. Maybe she's still there, and maybe not. We'll see."

As Rose Rita and Mrs. Zimmermann got closer to the store, they noticed a small black dog that was lying on the steps out in front. As soon as it saw them, it jumped to its feet and started to bark. Rose Rita was afraid it might try to bite them, but Mrs. Zimmermann was calm. She strode up to the steps, put her hands on her hips, and yelled, "Git!" The dog stood its ground and barked louder. Finally, just as Mrs. Zimmermann was getting ready to aim a good hard kick at the dog, it jumped sideways off the steps and ran off into the shrubbery at the end of the driveway.

"Dumb mutt," grumbled Mrs. Zimmermann. She walked up the steps and opened the door of the shop.

Ting-a-ling went the little bell. The lights in the shop were on, but there was no one behind the counter. Minutes passed as Mrs. Zimmermann and Rose Rita stood there waiting. Finally they began to hear some clumping and bumping around in the back of the shop. A door rattled open, and in walked Gert Bigger. She was a big rawboned woman in a shapeless sack of a dress, and she had an angry face. When she saw Mrs. Zimmermann, she looked startled.

"Oh, it's *you!* You haven't been up this way in quite a while. Well, what do you want?"

Gert Bigger sounded so nasty that Rose Rita wondered if maybe she had a grudge against Mrs. Zimmermann.

Mrs. Zimmermann answered in a quiet voice. "I'd just like some gas, if it won't trouble you too much. We ran out down the road a bit."

"Just a minute," snapped Gert.

She marched down the main aisle of the store and out the door, slamming it as she went.

"Gee, what an old crab!" said Rose Rita.

Mrs. Zimmermann shook her head sadly. "Yes, she gets worse every time I see her. Come on, let's get our gas and get out of here."

After a good deal of fussing around and cursing, Gert Bigger found a five-gallon gasoline can and filled it. Rose

Rita liked the smell of gasoline, and she liked to watch the numbers on the pump whirl. When the numbers stopped, Gert shut off the pump and announced the price. It was exactly twice what it said on the pump.

Mrs. Zimmermann looked hard at the woman. She was trying to figure out if Gert was kidding. "Are you having a little joke, Gertie? Look at those numbers there."

"It's no joke, dearie. Pay up, or you walk to the farm." She added, in a sneering voice, "It's my special price for friends."

Mrs. Zimmermann paused a minute, wondering what to do. Rose Rita was hoping she would wave her hand and turn Gert Bigger into a toad or something. Finally Mrs. Zimmermann heaved a deep sigh and opened her pocketbook. "There! Much good may it do you. Now come on, Rose Rita, let's get back to the car."

"Okay."

Mrs. Zimmermann picked up the gas can, and they started back down the road. After they had rounded the first bend, Rose Rita said, "What's the matter with that old lady, anyway? How come she's mad at you?"

"She's mad at everybody, Rosie. Mad at the world. I knew her when I was younger, back when I used to come up here and spend summers at the old farm. In fact one summer, when I was eighteen, she and I fought over the same boy friend, a guy named Mordecai Hunks.

I won the fight, but he and I didn't go together very long. We broke up at the end of the summer. I don't know who he married."

"Was Gertie mad at you for taking away her boy friend?"

Mrs. Zimmermann chuckled and shook her head. "You bet she was! And you know what? She's *still* mad! That woman is an expert grudge carrier. She remembers things people said years and years ago, and she's always planning to get even with somebody. I must say, though, that I've never seen her act quite the way she did tonight. I wonder what got into her?" Mrs. Zimmermann stopped in the middle of the road and turned. She looked back in the direction of Gert Bigger's store, and she rubbed her chin. She seemed to be thinking. Then, with a shrug, she turned and walked on toward the car.

It was dark now. Crickets chirped in the roadside weeds, and once a rabbit darted across their path and disappeared into the bushes on the other side. When Mrs. Zimmermann and Rose Rita finally got back to the car, it was sitting there in the moonlight, patiently waiting for them. Rose Rita had gotten to thinking of the car as a real person. For one thing, it had a face. The eyes were starey, like the eyes of cows, but the mouth was fishlike— mournful and heavy-lipped. The expression was sad, but dignified.

"The Plymouth is a nice car, isn't it?" said Rose Rita.

"Yes, I guess I'll have to admit that it is," said Mrs. Zimmermann, scratching her chin thoughtfully. "For a green car, it's not half bad."

"Can we give it a name?" said Rose Rita suddenly.

Mrs. Zimmermann looked startled. "Name? Well, yes, I suppose so. What kind of name would you like to give it?"

"Bessie." Rose Rita had once known a cow named Bessie. She thought Bessie would be a good name for this patient starey-eyed car.

Mrs. Zimmermann emptied the five-gallon can of gasoline into Bessie. When she turned the key in the ignition, the car started immediately. Rose Rita cheered. They were on their way again.

When they got to Mrs. Bigger's store, Mrs. Zimmermann stopped just long enough to stand the empty gas can next to the pumps. As the car chugged along toward the farm, Rose Rita noticed that the forest that ran behind Gert Bigger's store continued on down the road.

"That's a pretty big woods, isn't it, Mrs. Zimmermann?" she said, pointing off to the right.

"Uh-huh. It's a state forest, and as you say, a pretty big one. It runs all the way out to Oley's farm and then up north for quite a ways. It's a nice place, but I'd hate to get lost in it. You could wander around for days, and nobody'd find you."

They drove on. Rose Rita began to wonder what Oley's farm would be like. She had been daydreaming about the farm on the ride up, and she already had in her mind a very clear idea of what the place ought to look like. Would it really be that way? She'd see in a minute. Up a few hills, down a few hills, around a few curves, then down a long narrow rutty road overhung with trees. And then, suddenly, there was old Oley's farm.

It didn't look like Rose Rita's daydream, but it was nice. The barn was long and painted white. Like Bessie, it had a face: two windows for the eyes, and a tall door for a mouth. Near the barn stood the house. It was plain and square, with a square little cupola on top. The place looked totally deserted. Tall grass grew in the front yard, and the mailbox was beginning to get rusty. One of the windows in the barn was broken. As Rose Rita watched, a bird flew in through the hole. Off in the distance the forest could be seen.

Mrs. Zimmermann drove right up to the barn door and stopped. She got out and then, with Rose Rita's help, she rolled back the heavy door. A faint smell of manure and hay drifted out into the chilly air. There were two long rows of cattle stalls (both of them empty) and overhead Rose Rita could see hay. Some old license plates were nailed to the beams that supported the hay mow. When Rose Rita looked at them, she saw that they had dates like 1917 and 1923. Up among the rafters the shadowy form of a bird flew back and forth. Rose Rita and Mrs. Zimmermann stood there silent under the high roof. It was almost like being in church.

It was Mrs. Zimmermann who finally broke the spell. "Well, come on," she said. "Let's get the picnic hamper and the cooler and unlock the house. I'm starved."

"So am I," said Rose Rita. But when Mrs. Zimmermann opened the front door of the farmhouse and turned on the lights, she got a shock. The house looked as if a whirlwind had passed through it. Things were scattered everywhere. Drawers had been pulled out of dressers and cabinets, and the contents had been dumped out on the floor. Pictures had been taken down off the walls, and every book had been pulled out of a small narrow bookcase that stood in the front hall.

"Good Lord!" said Mrs. Zimmermann. "What on earth do you suppose . . ." She turned and looked at Rose Rita. They were both thinking the same thing.

Rose Rita followed Mrs. Zimmermann to the room that Oley Gunderson had used as his study. Against one wall of the room stood a massive roll-top desk. The top was rolled up, and all the cubbyholes at the back of the desk were empty. There were finger marks in the dust on the surface of the desk, and the pencils had been dumped out of the pencil jar. All the drawers of the desk had been pulled out and lay scattered around on the floor. The wood around the place where the bottom left-hand drawer had been was scarred and splintered— apparently it was the only drawer that had been locked. Near the desk lay a drawer with a badly chipped front, and in the drawer lay a Benrus watchcase covered with black leather.

Mrs. Zimmermann knelt down and picked up the watchcase. When she opened it, she found inside a small square ring box covered with blue velvet. Without a word, Mrs. Zimmermann opened the little blue box and looked inside. Rose Rita leaned over her shoulder to see.

The bottom half of the box held a black plush cushion with a slit in it. The slit appeared to have been widened, as if something too big for it had been crammed into the box. But whatever the something was, it was gone.

CHAPTER THREE

Mrs. Zimmermann knelt there on the littered floor, staring at the empty ring box. Suddenly she laughed.

"Ha! That's a good joke on whoever our burglar was!"

Rose Rita was dumbfounded. "I don't get what you mean, Mrs. Zimmermann."

Mrs. Zimmermann got up and brushed dust off her dress. She pitched the ring box contemptuously into the empty drawer. "It's all very simple, my dear. Don't you see? Oley must have blabbed around that ridiculous story about a magic ring. Someone must have believed him and figured that there was something valuable hidden here in the house. After all, you wouldn't have to think a ring was magic to want to steal it. Rings are usually made of precious metals, like gold and silver, and some of them are set with diamonds and rubies and suchlike. After Oley died, someone must have broken in. I can imagine what he found! Probably an old faucet washer. Well, it could be worse. They might have set fire to the place. The house is a mess though, and you and I will have to do some tidying up. Now then . . ."

Mrs. Zimmermann went on chattering as she straightened up Oley's desk, putting the pencils in the pencil jar and erasers into cubbyholes. Who the heck does she think she's fooling? Rose Rita thought. She could tell from the way Mrs. Zimmermann was acting that this was all just a cover-up. She had seen Mrs. Zimmermann's hand tremble as she opened the little box. She had seen how pale she looked. So there really is a magic ring, Rose Rita said to herself. I wonder what it looks like. She also wondered who had taken it, and what they were going to do with it. She had walked into a real live mystery, and she was so excited about the whole business that she really wasn't scared at all.

It was nearly midnight when Rose Rita and Mrs. Zimmermann finally sat down to have their picnic supper. They laid out their meal on the kitchen table and fetched some dusty plates and tarnished silverware from the cupboard over the sink. After that it was time to turn in. There were two adjoining bedrooms at the top of the stairs, each with its own small dark oak bedstead. Rose

Rita and Mrs. Zimmermann rummaged in a linen closet at the end of the hall, and they found some sheets. The sheets smelled musty, but they were clean. They made up their beds and said good night to each other.

Rose Rita had trouble getting to sleep. It was a hot still night, and not a breath of air was stirring. The curtains on the open window hung still. She tossed and turned, but it was no use. Finally Rose Rita sat up and turned on the lamp on the bedside table. She dug into her valise for the copy of *Treasure Island* that she had brought along to read, and she propped her pillow up against the head of the bed. Now then, where had she left off? Oh, sure. Here it was. Long John Silver had captured Jim, and they and the pirates were searching for Captain Flint's treasure. It was an exciting part of the book. Jim had a rope around his middle and was being dragged along over the sand by Silver, who swung along jauntily on his crutch . . .

Tap, tap, tap. As she read, Rose Rita began to be aware of a sound. At first she thought it was in her head. She often imagined sights and sounds and smells when she was reading, and now maybe she was imagining the sound of Long John Silver's crutch. *Tap, tap, tap, tap* . . . it didn't sound like that, though . . . more like a coin being rapped on a desk top . . . and anyway, a crutch wouldn't make any noise on the sand. It would just . . .

Rose Rita's head drooped forward. The book fell

from her hand. When she realized what was happening, she shook herself violently. What a dope I am for falling asleep, she thought at first, but then she remembered that she was trying to read herself to sleep. I guess it worked, Rose Rita thought, with a grin. *Tap, tap, tap.* There was that sound again. Where was it coming from? It certainly wasn't in her head. It was coming from Mrs. Zimmermann's room. And then Rose Rita knew what the sound was. It was Mrs. Zimmermann rapping her ring on something.

Mrs. Zimmermann had a ring with a large stone set in it. The stone was purple, because Mrs. Zimmermann loved purple things. It wasn't a magic ring, it was just a trinket that Mrs. Zimmermann liked. She had gotten it at Coney Island. She wore it all the time, and whenever she was thinking about something, thinking really hard, she rapped the ring on whatever happened to be around, chairs or tabletops or bookshelves. The door was closed between the two rooms, but Rose Rita could see, in her mind's eye, a clear picture of Mrs. Zimmermann lying awake, staring at the ceiling and rapping her ring against the sideboard of the bed. What was she thinking about? The ring, probably—the other ring, the stolen one. Rose Rita really wanted to go in and talk the whole matter over with Mrs. Zimmermann, but she knew that was not the thing to do. Mrs. Zimmermann would shut up like a clam if Rose Rita tried to talk to her about Oley Gunderson's magic ring.

Rose Rita shrugged her shoulders and sighed. There was nothing she could do, and anyway she was nearly asleep. She fluffed her pillow up, turned out the light, and stretched out. In no time at all, she was snoring peacefully.

The next morning, bright and early, Rose Rita and Mrs. Zimmermann got their things together, locked up the house, and drove off toward Petoskey. They had breakfast in a café there and went to see Oley's lawyer. Then they drove on toward the Straits. That afternoon they crossed the Straits of Mackinac in a car ferry called *The City of Escanaba*. The sky was gray, and it was raining. The ferryboat heaved ponderously in the choppy waters of the Straits. Off on their right Mrs. Zimmermann and Rose Rita could just barely see Mackinac Island, a gray blurry smudge. The sun was coming out when *The City of Escanaba* reached St. Ignace. They were in the Upper Peninsula of Michigan now, and they were going to have two whole weeks to explore it.

The trip started off well. They saw Tahquamenon Falls and drove along the shore of Lake Superior. They saw the Pictured Rocks and snapped photos of each other. They drove through rolling oceans of pine trees and stopped to look at streams that ran red because there was so much iron in the water. They visited towns with strange names, like Ishpeming and Germfask and Ontonagon. At night they stayed in tourist homes. Mrs. Zimmermann hated the new motels that were springing up all over the place, but she loved tourist homes. Old white houses on shady back streets, houses with screened porches and green shutters and sagging trellises with morning glories or hollyhocks on them. Mrs. Zimmermann and Rose Rita would settle down for the night in a tourist home and sit out on the porch playing chess or cards and drinking iced tea while the crickets chirped outside. Sometimes there was a radio in Rose Rita's room. If there was, she would listen to the Detroit Tigers' night games until she got sleepy. And then in the morning breakfast in a diner or café, and then back on the road again.

On the fourth day of their trip something odd happened.

It was evening. Rose Rita and Mrs. Zimmermann were walking down the main street of a little town. The sun was setting at the end of the street, and a hot orange light lay on everything. They had had their dinner and were just stretching their legs after a long day of driving. Rose Rita was ready to go back to the tourist home, but Mrs. Zimmermann had stopped to look in the window of a junk shop. She loved to browse in junk shops. She could spend hours sifting through all sorts of trash, and sometimes she had to be dragged away by force.

As she stood by the window, Mrs. Zimmermann

noticed that the store was open. It was nine o'clock at night, but the owners of junk shops often keep odd hours. She went in, and Rose Rita followed her. There were old chairs with ratty velvet upholstery, and bookcases with a few books in them, and old dining room tables with an incredible assortment of junk laid out on them. Mrs. Zimmermann stopped in front of one of these tables. She picked up a salt and pepper set shaped like a fielder's mitt and a ball. The ball was the salt.

"How'd you like this for your room, Rose Rita?" she said, chuckling.

Rose Rita said she would love it. She liked anything that had to do with baseball. "Gee, could I have it for my desk, Mrs. Zimmermann? I think it's kind of cute."

"Okay," said Mrs. Zimmermann, still laughing. She paid the owner twenty-five cents for the set and went on browsing. Next to a dusty bowl full of mother-of-pearl buttons was a stack of old photographs. They were all printed on heavy cardboard, and, from the clothes that people in the pictures were wearing, they must have been pretty old. Humming, Mrs. Zimmermann shuffled through the stack. Suddenly she gasped.

Rose Rita, who had been standing nearby, turned and looked at Mrs. Zimmermann. Her face was pale, and the hand that held the photograph was trembling.

"What's wrong, Mrs. Zimmermann?"

"Come . . . come over here, Rose Rita, and look at this."

Rose Rita went to Mrs. Zimmermann's side and looked at the picture she was holding. It showed a woman in an old-fashioned floor-length dress. She was standing by the bank of a river, and she had a canoe paddle in her hand. Behind her a canoe was pulled up on the bank. A man in a striped jacket was sitting cross-legged next to the canoe. He had a handlebar mustache, and he was playing a banjo. The man looked handsome, but it was impossible to tell what the lady looked like. Someone had scraped the face of the lady away with a knife or a razor blade.

Rose Rita still didn't see what was bothering Mrs. Zimmermann. But as she stood there wondering, Mrs. Zimmermann turned the picture over. On the back these words were written: *Florence and Mordecai. Summer, 1905.*

"My gosh!" exclaimed Rose Rita. "Is that a picture of you?"

Mrs. Zimmermann nodded. "It is. Or rather, was, until someone . . . did that to it." She swallowed hard.

"How the heck did a picture of you get way up here, Mrs. Zimmermann? Did you used to live up here?"

"No, I did not. I've never seen this town in my life before. It's all . . . well, it's all very strange."

Mrs. Zimmermann's voice shook as she spoke. Rose Rita could see very clearly that she was upset. Mrs. Zimmermann was the sort of person who usually gave you the feeling that she had everything under control. She was a calm sensible sort. So when she got upset, you knew there was a reason.

Mrs. Zimmermann bought the photograph from the old man in the shop and took it back to the tourist home with her. On the way she explained to Rose Rita that witches and warlocks hacked up pictures that way when they wanted to get rid of somebody. Sometimes they let water drip on the photo until the face was worn away; or they might scrape the face off with a knife. Either way, it was like making a wax doll of somebody and sticking pins in it. It was a way of murdering somebody by magic.

Rose Rita's eyes opened wide. "You mean somebody's trying to do something to you?"

Mrs. Zimmermann laughed nervously. "No, no. I don't mean that at all. This whole thing, finding the picture of myself up here and finding it . . . damaged, well it's all just a funny coincidence. But when you fool around with magic the way I do, well, you get some strange ideas into your head. I mean, sometimes you have to be careful."

Rose Rita blinked. "I don't get what you mean."

"I mean I'm going to burn the picture," Mrs. Zimmermann snapped. "Now, I'd rather not talk about it any more, if you don't mind."

Late that night Rose Rita lay in bed, trying to sleep. Mrs. Zimmermann was downstairs in the guest parlor, reading—at least that's what she was supposed to be doing. On a hunch Rose Rita got up and went to the window. She remembered that she had seen an incinerator in the back yard. Sure enough, there was Mrs. Zimmermann, standing over the wire incinerator. Something was burning with a soft red glow at the bottom of the cage. Mrs. Zimmermann stood hunched over, watching it. The reddish light flickered over her face. Rose Rita felt afraid. She went back to bed and tried to sleep, but the picture of Mrs. Zimmermann standing there over her fire, like a witch in an old story, kept coming back to her. What was going on?

CHAPTER FOUR

The next morning at breakfast Rose Rita tried to get Mrs. Zimmermann to talk about the photograph, but Mrs. Zimmermann rather curtly told her to mind her own business. This of course made Rose Rita more curious than ever, but her curiosity wasn't getting her anywhere. The mystery would have to remain a mystery, at least for the time being.

A few days later Rose Rita and Mrs. Zimmermann were in a town over near the Wisconsin border. Once again they had settled down in a tourist home for the night. Rose Rita went out to mail a couple of postcards, and on her way back she happened to pass a high school gym where a Saturday night dance was in full swing. It was a hot night, and the doors of the gym were open. Rose Rita stopped a minute in the doorway and looked in at the kids who were moving slowly around on the dance floor. A big ball covered with little mirrors revolved overhead, scattering coins of light on the dancers below. The room was softly lit with blue and red light. Rose Rita stood and stared. It was really a beautiful scene, and she found herself thinking that maybe going to dances would be fun. But then she glanced along the wall and noticed some girls standing by the sidelines. No one was dancing with them. They were just standing there, watching. It didn't look like they were having a very good time.

A wave of sadness swept over Rose Rita. She felt tears stinging her eyes. Would she be in that wallflower line next year? It would be better to climb on a train and ride out to California and be a hobo. Did they let girls be hoboes? Come to think of it, she had never heard of a girl hobo. What a lousy deal girls had, anyway! They couldn't even be bums if they wanted to.

Rose Rita felt angry all the rest of the way home. She stomped up the steps of the tourist home and slammed the screen door behind her. There on the porch sat Mrs. Zimmermann. She was playing solitaire. As soon as she saw Rose Rita, she knew something was wrong.

"What's the matter, my dear? Is the world getting to be too much for you?"

"Yeah," said Rose Rita sullenly. "Can I sit down and talk to you?"

"Sure thing," said Mrs. Zimmermann as she gathered the cards into a heap. "This was getting to be a pretty dull game, anyway. What's on your mind?"

Rose Rita sat down on the glider, swung back and forth a bit, and then said abruptly, "If I keep on being friends with Lewis, am I gonna have to go out on dates with him and go to dances and all that stuff?"

Mrs. Zimmermann looked a bit startled. She stared off into space for a minute and thought. "No," she said slowly, as she rocked to and fro on the glider. "No, I don't see that you have to do that. Not if you don't want to. You like Lewis as a friend and not because he shows up at your door with a bunch of flowers in his hand. I think it should probably stay that way."

"Gee, you're great, Mrs. Zimmermann!" said Rose Rita, grinning. "I wish you'd talk to my mom. She thinks Lewis and I are gonna get married next year or something."

Mrs. Zimmermann made a sour face. "If I talked to your mother, it would make things worse, not better," she said, as she started laying out another hand of solitaire. "Your mother wouldn't like it much if I started butting in on her family's business. Besides, she may be right. In ninety-eight percent of the cases, a friendship like yours and Lewis's either breaks up or turns into a dating friendship. You may discover next year that you and Lewis are going different ways."

"But I don't want that to happen," said Rose Rita

stubbornly. "I like Lewis. I like him a whole lot. I just want things to stay the way they are."

"Ah, but that's just the trouble!" said Mrs. Zimmermann. "Things *don't* stay the same. They keep changing. You're changing, and so is Lewis. Who knows what you and he will think six months from now, or a year from now?"

Rose Rita thought a bit. "Yeah," she said at last, "but what if Lewis and me just decided to be friends the rest of our lives? What if I never got married, not ever? Would people think I was an old maid?"

Mrs. Zimmermann picked up the deck of cards and began to shuffle it slowly. "Well," she said thoughtfully, "some people would say that I've been leading the life of an old maid for some years now. Since my husband died, I mean. Most women would've remarried, quick as anything, but when Honus died, I decided to try single life—widowhood, call it what you like—for a while. And you know, it's not so bad. Of course, it helps to have friends like Jonathan. But the point I'm trying to make is, there isn't any one way of doing things that's the best. I was happy as a wife, and I'm happy as a widow. So try different things. See what you like best. There are people, of course, who can only do one thing, who can only function in one kind of situation. But I think they're pretty sad people, and I'd hate to think you were one of them."

Mrs. Zimmermann stopped talking and stared off into

space. Rose Rita sat there, with her mouth open, waiting for her to say more. But she said nothing. And when she turned and saw the anxious way Rose Rita was looking at her, she laughed.

"I'm through with my sermon," she chuckled. "And if you think I'm going to give you a handy-dandy recipe for how to live your life, you're crazy. Come on. How about a quick game or two of cribbage before bedtime? Okay?"

"You're on," said Rose Rita, grinning.

Mrs. Zimmermann got out her cribbage board, and she and Rose Rita played cribbage till it was time to go to bed. Then they went upstairs. As always there were two adjoining rooms, one for Rose Rita and one for Mrs. Zimmermann. Rose Rita washed her face and brushed her teeth. She threw herself down on the bed, and she was asleep almost before her head hit the pillow.

Later that night, around two in the morning, Rose Rita woke up. She woke up with the feeling that something was wrong. Very wrong. But when she sat up and looked around, the room looked absolutely peaceful. The reflection of the moon floated in the mirror over the bureau, and the streetlamp outside cast a puzzly black-and-white map on the closet door. Rose Rita's clothes lay neatly piled on the chair next to her bed. What was wrong then?

Well, something was. Rose Rita could feel it. She felt tense and prickly, and she could hear her heart beating

fast. Slowly she peeled back the sheet and got out of bed. It took her several minutes, but she finally got up the courage to go to the closet and yank the door open. There was a wild jangling of hangers. Rose Rita gave a nervous little yelp and jumped back. There was no one in the closet.

Rose Rita heaved a sigh of relief. Now she was beginning to feel silly. She was behaving like one of those little old ladies who peek under their beds every night before they turn out the lights. But as she was about to get back into bed, Rose Rita heard a noise. It came from the next room, and when she heard it, all her fear came rushing back. Oh come on, Rose Rita whispered to herself. Don't be such a scaredy-cat! But she couldn't just go back to bed. She had to go look.

The door between Mrs. Zimmermann's room and Rose Rita's room was ajar. Rose Rita crept slowly toward it and laid her hand on the knob. She pushed, and the door moved softly inward. Rose Rita froze. There was somebody standing by Mrs. Zimmermann's bed. For a long second, Rose Rita stared wide-eyed and rigid with terror. Suddenly she gave a wild yell and leaped into the room. The door crashed against the wall, and somehow Rose Rita's hand found the light switch. The bulb in the ceiling flashed on, and Mrs. Zimmermann sat up, disheveled and blinking. But there was no one standing by the bed. No one at all.

CHAPTER FIVE

Mrs. Zimmermann rubbed her eyes. Around her lay the rumpled bedclothes, and at the foot of the bed stood Rose Rita, who looked stunned.

"Good heavens, Rose Rita!" exclaimed Mrs. Zimmermann. "Is this some kind of new game? What on earth are you doing in here?"

Rose Rita's head was in a whirl. She began to wonder whether she might be losing her mind. She had been sure, absolutely sure, that she had seen someone moving about near the head of Mrs. Zimmermann's bed. "Gee, I'm sorry, Mrs. Zimmermann," she said. "I'm really awfully sorry, really I am! I thought I saw somebody in here."

Mrs. Zimmermann cocked her head to one side and

curled up the corner of her mouth. "My dear," she said dryly, "you have been reading too many Nancy Drew novels. What you probably saw was my dress on this chair. The window is open, and it must have been fluttering in the breeze. Now go back to bed, for heaven's sake! We both need some more shut-eye if we're to go gallivanting all over the Upper Peninsula tomorrow."

Rose Rita stared at the chair that stood next to Mrs. Zimmermann's bed. A purple dress hung limply from the chair's back. It was a hot still night. Not a breath of air was stirring. Rose Rita did not see how she could possibly have mistaken the dress on the chair for somebody moving around in the room. But then what had she seen? She didn't know. Bewildered and ashamed, Rose Rita backed toward the door. "G-good night, Mrs. Zimmermann," she stammered. "I . . . I'm really sorry I woke you up."

Mrs. Zimmermann smiled kindly at Rose Rita. She shrugged her shoulders. "It's okay, Rosie. No harm done. I've had some pretty wild nightmares in my time. Why, I remember one where . . . but never mind. I'll tell you some other time. Good night now, and sleep tight."

"I will." Rose Rita turned out the light and went back to her own room. She lay down on the bed, but she didn't go to sleep. She put her hands up behind her head and stared at the ceiling. She was worried. First there had been that photograph, and now this. Something was happening. Something was going on, but she couldn't for the life of her figure out what. And then there was that business of the break-in at Oley's farm, and the empty ring box. Did that have anything to do with what had happened tonight? Rose Rita thought and thought, but she didn't come up with any answers. It was like having two or three pieces of a large and complicated jigsaw puzzle. The pieces didn't make any sense all by themselves. Rose Rita figured that Mrs. Zimmermann must be as worried as she was. In fact, she was probably more worried, since the strange things were happening to her. Of course, Mrs. Zimmermann would never let on that she was upset. She was always ready to help other people, but she kept her own problems to herself. That was her way. Rose Rita bit her lip. She felt helpless. And she had a strong feeling that something really bad was going to happen soon. What would it be? That was another thing she didn't know.

Next day, toward evening, Mrs. Zimmermann and Rose Rita were bumping along a rutty back road about twenty miles from the town of Ironwood. They had been driving for about an hour on this road, and now they were about ready to turn back. Mrs. Zimmerman had wanted Rose Rita to see an abandoned copper mine that had once belonged to a friend of her family. At every turn in the road she had expected to see it. But the mine never appeared, and now Mrs. Zimmermann was getting discouraged.

The road was just plain awful. Bessie jounced and

jiggled so much that Rose Rita felt as if she were inside a Mixmaster. Every now and then the car would go banging down into a pothole, or a rock would fly up and hit the underside of the car with a sound like a muffled bell. And it was another hot day. Sweat was pouring down Rose Rita's face, and her glasses kept getting fogged up. Sandflies buzzed in and out of the open windows of the car. They kept trying to bite Rose Rita on the arms, and she slapped at them till her arms stung.

Finally Mrs. Zimmermann put on the brakes. She turned off the motor and said, "Darn it all anyway! I did want to show you that mine, but it must have been on another road. We'd better turn back if we're going to . . . oh, Oh Lord!"

Mrs. Zimmermann clutched the steering wheel and doubled over. Her knuckles showed white under her skin, and her face was twisted with pain. She clutched at her stomach. "My . . . God!" she gasped. "I've . . . never . . ." She winced and closed her eyes. When she was able to speak again, her voice was barely a whisper. "Rose Rita?"

Rose Rita was terrified. She sat on the edge of her seat and watched Mrs. Zimmermann. "Yeah, Mrs. Zimmermann? What . . . what's the matter? What happened? Are you okay?"

Mrs. Zimmermann managed a feeble smile. "No, I'm not okay," she croaked. "I think I have appendicitis."

"Oh my gosh!" When Rose Rita was in the fourth

grade, a kid in her class had died of appendicitis. His folks had just thought that he had a bad stomachache until it was too late. Then his appendix broke open, and he died. Rose Rita felt panicky. "Oh my gosh!" she said, again. "Mrs. Zimmermann, what are we gonna do?"

"We . . . we have to get me to a hospital quick," Mrs. Zimmermann said. "The only catch is . . . oh. Oh no, please no!" Mrs. Zimmermann bent over again, writhing with pain. Tears streamed down her face, and she bit her lip so hard that it bled. "The only catch . . ." Mrs. Zimmermann gasped, when she could talk again, ". . . the only catch is that I don't think I can drive."

Rose Rita sat perfectly still and stared at the dashboard. When she spoke, her lips barely moved. "I . . . I think I can, Mrs. Zimmermann."

Mrs. Zimmermann closed her eyes as another wave of pain swept over her. "What . . . what did you say?"

"I said, I think maybe I could drive. I learned to, once."

Rose Rita was not exactly telling the truth. About a year ago she had gone out to visit a cousin of hers who lived on a farm near New Zebedee. He was fourteen, and he knew how to drive a tractor. Rose Rita had pestered him until he finally agreed to teach her how to shift gears and let the clutch in and out. He taught her on an old wrecked car that sat in a field near the farmhouse, and after he had showed her the ropes, Rose Rita practiced by herself until she had all the gear positions straight in her head. But she had never actually been behind the wheel of a moving car, or even a car that just had the motor running.

Mrs. Zimmermann said nothing. But she motioned for Rose Rita to get out of the car. When she did, Mrs. Zimmermann dragged herself over into the seat where Rose Rita had been and slumped there against the door with her hand on her stomach. Rose Rita walked around and got in on the driver's side. She shut the door and sat there staring at the wheel. She was afraid, but a voice inside of her said, Come on. You've got to do it. She can't, she's too sick. Come on, Rose Rita.

Rose Rita slid forward until she was sitting on the edge of the seat. She would have moved the seat up, but she was afraid it would hurt Mrs. Zimmermann. Fortunately Rose Rita was tall for thirteen, and she had grown a lot in the past year. Her legs were long enough for her to reach the pedals. Rose Rita tapped the accelerator cautiously. Could she really do it? Well, she'd have to try.

Mrs. Zimmermann had left the car in first gear. But you couldn't start a car when it was in first gear, it had to be in neutral. At least that was what Rose Rita had heard from her cousin. Cautiously she pushed the clutch pedal in and eased the lever up into neutral. She turned the ignition key, and the car started instantly. Now, with her right foot on the gas and her left on the clutch, she pulled the gear shift lever forward and down. Slowly she began to let the clutch out the way she had been taught to do it. The car shuddered, and the engine killed.

"You've . . . got to . . . give it the . . . gas," Mrs. Zimmermann gasped. "When you . . . let the clutch out. . . give 'er the gun."

"Okay." Rose Rita was tense and trembling all over. She put the car back in neutral and started it up again. This time when she let the clutch out, she really floored the gas pedal. The car took a little jump forward and stopped again. Apparently too much gas was just as bad as too little. Rose Rita turned to ask Mrs. Zimmermann what to do now, but Mrs. Zimmermann had passed out. She was on her own.

Rose Rita gritted her teeth. She was getting mad now. "Okay, we're gonna try again," she said in a quiet firm voice. She tried and again the motor killed. It killed the next time, too. But the time after that she managed, somehow, to let the clutch out and press the gas pedal at just the right rate. The car moved slowly forward.

"*Yay, Bessie!*" Rose Rita yelled. She yelled so loud that Mrs. Zimmermann opened her eyes. She blinked and smiled feebly when she saw that the car was moving. "Atta girl, Rosie!" she whispered. Then she slumped over sideways and lost consciousness again.

Somehow Rose Rita managed to get the car turned around and headed back toward Ironwood. It was dark now, and she had to turn the lights on. The road was totally deserted. No farms, no homes. Rose Rita remembered one ruined shanty that they had passed, but it didn't seem likely that there was anyone living in it. No. Unless a car just happened to come along, there would be no help until they reached the two-lane blacktop that led back to Ironwood. Rose Rita swallowed hard. If she could just keep the car going, maybe everything would turn out all right. She glanced quickly at Mrs. Zimmermann. She lay slumped against the door. Her eyes were closed, and every now and then she would moan faintly. Rose Rita clenched her teeth and drove.

On Bessie crawled, up and down hills, over bumps and rocks, and in and out of potholes. Her pale headlight beams reached out before her into the night. Moths and other night insects fluttered past. Rose Rita felt as if she were driving along in a dark tunnel. Dark pine trees lined the road on either side. They seemed to press forward until Rose Rita felt hemmed in. An owl was hooting in the woods somewhere. Rose Rita felt lonely and frightened. She wanted to drive fast to get out of this awful place, but she was scared to. The road was so bumpy that she was afraid to speed up. It was frightening to have a big heavy car under her control. Every time the car hit a pothole, the wheel lurched violently to the right or the left. Somehow, though, each time Rose Rita managed to get straightened out. Oh, please, she prayed, get us there, Bessie. Please get us there before Mrs. Zimmermann dies. Please . . .

Rose Rita was not sure when, but after she had driven

along the dark winding road for some time, she began to have the feeling that there was someone else in the car with them. Rose Rita didn't know why she had this feeling, but it was there, and it was very persistent. She kept glancing up toward the rear-view mirror, but she never saw anything. After a while the feeling got to be so maddening that Rose Rita stopped the car. She put it in neutral, pulled on the emergency brake, and, as the car throbbed, she turned on the overhead light and glanced nervously into the back seat. It was empty. Rose Rita flipped off the light, put the car back in gear, and drove on. But the feeling kept coming back, and she found that it took a strong effort of the will to keep her eyes from wandering toward the rear-view mirror. The car was rounding a sharp curve when Rose Rita happened to glance up, and she saw, reflected in the mirror, the shadow of a head and two glittering eyes.

Rose Rita screamed and jerked the wheel violently to the left. With a screech of tires, Bessie swerved off the road and plunged down a steep bank. The car bounced and jounced wildly, and Mrs. Zimmermann's inert body slammed first against the door and then slid over across the seat to bump against Rose Rita. Rose Rita, panic-stricken, clutched the wheel and kept trying to find the brake with her foot, but she kept missing it. Down into darkness they went. Now there was a loud swishing, crackling sound outside the car, and a funny smell. In the fevered whirling of her brain Rose Rita found her-

self wondering, What is that smell? The crackling and swishing got louder, and finally Rose Rita got her foot on the brake. Her body lurched forward, and her head hit the windshield. She blacked out.

CHAPTER SIX

Rose Rita dreamed that she was clinging to a piece of wood that was floating in the sea. Someone was saying to her, "Are you all right? Are you all right?" That's a dumb thing to be saying, thought Rose Rita. Then she opened her eyes and found that she was sitting at the wheel of Bessie. A policeman was standing next to the car. He reached in the open window and touched her gently.

"Are you okay, miss?"

Rose Rita shook her head groggily. She touched her forehead and felt a swelling lump. "Yeah, I guess so, except for this bump on my head. I . . . my gosh! What happened?" She looked around, and saw that the car was embedded in a large clump of juniper bushes. Juniper! That was the smell! Daylight was streaming in through the dusty windows of the car. And there, on the seat beside her, lay Mrs. Zimmermann. She was asleep. Or was she . . . ?

Rose Rita reached over and started shaking Mrs. Zimmermann's shoulder. "Wake up, Mrs. Zimmermann!" she sobbed. "Oh, please! Wake up, wake—"

Rose Rita felt the policeman's firm hand on her arm. "Better not do that, miss. You don't know if she's got any broken bones or not. We've got an ambulance coming, and they'll check her over before they try to move her. What happened? Fall asleep at the wheel?"

Rose Rita shook her head. "I was trying to drive Mrs. Zimmermann back to the hospital after she got sick all of a sudden. I got scared and I drove off the road. I'm only thirteen, and I don't have any license. Are you gonna put me in jail?"

The policeman smiled sadly at Rose Rita. "No, ma'am. Not this time, anyway. But I think it wasn't very bright of you to try to drive, even if it was an emergency and all. You might of gotten yourself killed. As a matter of fact, if these bushes hadn't of been here, you *would've* been killed. And so would your friend there. But she's breathin' okay. I looked at her a minute ago. All we have to do is sit tight till the ambulance gets here."

A little while later a big white ambulance with a red cross on the side pulled up on the road next to the police car. Two men in white uniforms got out and edged their way down the embankment. They had a stretcher with them. By the time they got to the car, Mrs. Zimmermann was just coming to. The two men checked her over, and when they were sure she could be moved, they gently eased her out of the car and made her lie down on the stretcher. Up the hill they went with her, slowly. When they had her safe in the ambulance, they went back for Rose Rita. It turned out that she was a little bruised and shaken up, but otherwise okay. She climbed the hill on her own and got in the back of the ambulance with Mrs. Zimmermann. Off they went, siren screaming, toward Ironwood.

Mrs. Zimmermann spent the next three days in the hospital at Ironwood. The mysterious pains never returned, and the doctors informed her that they had been in the wrong part of the body for appendicitis. Mrs. Zimmermann was puzzled and frightened. Somehow it was worse not to know what had caused the pains, and the thought that they might return at any time was enough to make her very nervous. It was like living with a time bomb that might or might not go off.

So Mrs. Zimmermann, much as she disliked the idea, stayed in bed while the doctors at the hospital ran a series of tests. Nurses stuck needles into her and drew blood. They gave her vile-tasting potions to drink and made marks on charts. She was x-rayed and put in front of, and inside of, all sorts of strange science-fiction machines. Doctors stopped by every now and then to talk with Mrs. Zimmermann, but they never told her anything that she wanted to know.

Meanwhile, Rose Rita became a lodger at the hospital. Mrs. Zimmermann explained the situation to the doctors, and she showed them her insurance policy (which she always carried around with her in her purse, just in case), and it clearly stated that she was entitled to a private room. The private room had two beds, and Rose Rita slept in one of them. She played cards and chess with Mrs. Zimmermann and listened to night games with her on the radio. It so happened that the White Sox were playing at Detroit, and Mrs. Zimmermann was a White Sox fan because she had once lived in Chicago. So Rose Rita and she had fun rooting for opposite sides, and they even argued a bit, though not very seriously.

Some of the time, when sitting around in the hospital room got to be dull, Rose Rita went out and wandered around the town of Ironwood. She went to the public library and a Saturday afternoon movie. Some of the time she just explored. She got lost once or twice, but people were very nice to her, and she always managed to find her way back to the hospital.

On the afternoon of Mrs. Zimmermann's third day in the hospital, Rose Rita happened to be passing a vacant lot where some boys were playing move-up. They were getting tired of move-up, but they didn't have enough for teams. When they saw Rose Rita, they asked her if she wanted to play.

"I sure do!" Rose Rita yelled. "But whatever side gets me, they have to let me pitch."

The boys looked at each other for a minute, but after a hurried consultation, they decided that Rose Rita could pitch if she wanted to. Rose Rita loved to play baseball, and she really loved to pitch. She was the only girl in her school who could throw a curve with a softball. She had hesitation pitches, and blooper pitches, and she even had a knuckle ball, though it didn't work very well, because it's hard to hold a softball with your knuckles. Her underhand fast ball was famous—so famous, in fact, that she usually had to be persuaded just to lob it up there to weak hitters so they wouldn't strike out all the time.

So Rose Rita wound up playing softball with a bunch of boys she had never seen before. She got a lot of hits, and she grabbed off some hard line drives with her bare hands. She pitched, and she pitched pretty well until she happened to strike out a big husky kid with a crew cut. He thought he was a pretty good ball player, and he didn't like getting struck out by a girl. So he started getting on Rose Rita. He did all sorts of things: he kept calling her Four Eyes, and whenever her team took the field, he went out of his way to run past her just so he could give her a good hard shove and say "Oops, parm me, lady!" in a nasty sneering tone of voice. Finally, near the end of the game, Rose Rita hit a long drive that looked like it would be good for three bases. But as she dived into third, headfirst, there was the lug with the crew cut, and he had the ball in his hand. He could have tagged her on the shoulder or the arm or the back, but he shoved the ball right square into her mouth. It really hurt. The game stopped while Rose Rita pulled herself together. She checked her front teeth to make sure they weren't loose and cautiously rubbed her swollen upper lip. She felt like crying, but she fought down the urge. After a few minutes, Rose Rita went on playing.

In the ninth inning, when the crew-cut lug was pitching for the other side, Rose Rita hit a bases-loaded home run and won the game for her team. When she crossed home plate, all the boys on her side gathered around her and yelled "Yay, Rose Rita!" three times. It really made her feel great. But then she noticed that the guy who had been calling her names was standing there on the pitcher's mound and glaring straight at her.

"Hey, Four Eyes!" he yelled. "You think you're really somethin', doncha?"

"Yeah, I do," Rose Rita yelled back. "What's it to you?"

"Nothin' much. Hey, Four Eyes. How much do you know about baseball? Huh?"

"A heck of a lot more than you do," Rose Rita snapped.

"Oh yeah? Prove it."

"Whattaya mean, prove it?"

"I mean, let's have a contest to see who knows more about baseball, huh? How about it? You chicken? Chick-chick-chick, chick-chick-chick!" The boy flapped his arms like wings and did a rather poor imitation of a chicken.

Rose Rita grinned. This was too big a chance to miss. It so happened that Rose Rita was a real baseball nut. She knew all sorts of facts about baseball, like Ty Cobb's lifetime average and the number of unassisted triple plays that there were on record. She even knew about Smead Jolley's great record, four errors on a single played ball. So she figured that she would give this wiseacre kid a beating at the baseball fact game and get even with him for the fat lip he had given her.

Everybody gathered around to watch the contest. One of the other boys, a watery-eyed blond kid who talked through his nose, was chosen to think up questions. At first it was a pretty tough battle. The lug turned out to be pretty good at baseball facts. He knew the strikeout kings, and who the last thirty-game winner had been, and a lot of other stuff. But Rose Rita knew the stuff that the lug knew, so it turned into a tense nasty grudge fight that went on for some time, with neither one able to gain an inch on the other. In the end Rose Rita won, because she knew that Bill Wambsganss of the Cleveland Indians had pulled the only unassisted triple play ever to be pulled during a World Series game. The lug had a chance at the question first, but he didn't know the answer. Then it was Rose Rita's turn, and she knew it right away. Several of the boys yelled "Yay, Rose Rita!" and one even ran up to shake her hand.

The lug just got red in the face. He glowered at Rose Rita. If he had been mad before, he was furious now. "You think you're pretty damn smart, doncha?" he snarled.

"Yeah," said Rose Rita happily.

The lug put his hands on his hips and looked her straight in the eye. "Well, you wanna know what I think? I think you're a pretty funny kind of girl, that's what I think. A pret-ty damn funny kind of a girl."

It was a stupid remark, but it stung Rose Rita. It stung like a slap in the face. To the amazement of everyone, she burst into tears and ran off the field. *You're a pretty funny kind of a girl.* Rose Rita had heard people say this about her before, and what was worse, she had thought it about herself. She had often wondered if there was really something wrong with her. She acted like a boy, but she was a girl. Her best friend was a boy, but most of the girls she knew had girls for best friends. She didn't want to go on dates, even though some of the girls she knew had already started to date and had told her how much fun it was. A funny kind of a girl—Rose Rita couldn't get the phrase out of her head.

Rose Rita stopped on a street corner. She took out her hanky and dabbed at her eyes, and then she blew her nose. From the way people were looking at her as they passed by, she figured she must really be a mess. Her face felt hot and flushed. Now she was mad at herself, mad because she had let that dumb guy get her goat that way. As she walked along, she told herself that she had a lot to feel good about: she had practically won the game single-handed for her team, and she had won the baseball facts contest, in spite of what happened later. She started to whistle, and after two or three blocks of whistling, she felt better. She decided to go back to the hospital, just to see what was going on.

When Rose Rita walked into Mrs. Zimmermann's room, she walked in on an argument. Mrs. Zimmermann was sitting up in bed, and she was having it out with a worried-looking young doctor.

"But Mrs. Zimmermann," the doctor pleaded, "you're taking an *awful* chance with your health! If we had another day or so, we might be able to figure out—"

Mrs. Zimmermann cut him off contemptuously. "Oh, sure! If I were to stay here for a year, and if I were to lie very, very still, I'd get bedsores, and you'd know what to do about them, wouldn't you? Well, I'm sorry. I've wasted too much time as it is. Tomorrow morning, Rose Rita and I are hitting the road. You're just a bunch of quacks here, like most doctors."

"Now, Mrs. Zimmermann, I resent that. We've tried very hard to be nice to you, and we've also tried to find out about your pains. Just because all our tests have come out negative is no reason to . . ."

The doctor went on, and then Mrs. Zimmermann started in again. Rose Rita sat down in an armchair and hid behind a copy of *Ladies Home Journal*. She hoped that they wouldn't notice her. The argument went on for some time, and the doctor pleaded, and Mrs. Zimmermann was about as nasty and insulting as Rose Rita had ever seen her be. In the end Mrs. Zimmermann won. The doctor agreed that she could leave tomorrow morning if she wanted to.

Mrs. Zimmermann watched as the doctor gathered up his clip board, his stethoscope, and his medicine bag. When the door had closed behind him, she raised her hand and motioned for Rose Rita to come over to the bed.

"Rose Rita," she said. "We're in trouble."

"Huh?"

"I said, we're in trouble. I sent my dress out to be dry-cleaned. You know the one—the dress I was wearing when those pains hit me. The same dress that was draped over the chair by my bed, the night you thought you saw someone in my room. Remember?"

Rose Rita nodded.

"Well, the dress came back today, and look what came with it." Mrs. Zimmermann opened a drawer in the table that stood by the side of her bed. She took out a small brown Manila envelope and shook the contents out into Rose Rita's hand. Rose Rita looked down and saw a small golden safety pin and a little strip of paper.

There was writing in red ink on the paper, but she couldn't read it.

"What's this?"

"It's a charm. The cleaners found it pinned to the inside of my dress. Don't worry—it can't hurt you. Those things can only be rigged up to work on one person at a time."

"You . . . you mean . . ."

"Yes, my dear. That little strip of paper caused the pains I had the other night." Mrs. Zimmermann laughed grimly. "I wonder what Doc Smartypants there would say if I told him about *that!* I'm sorry, by the way, that I was so mean to him, but I had to be, so he'd let us go."

Rose Rita was frightened. She put the strip of paper and the pin on the table and backed away. "Mrs. Zimmermann," she said, "what are we gonna do?"

"I don't know, Rose Rita, I just don't know. Somebody is after me—that much is clear. But who it is or why they're doing it, I just don't know. I have some ideas, but I'd rather not share them with you right now, if you don't mind. I've told you all this because I don't want you to feel guilty about driving off the road that night. You had every right to be scared. The thing you saw in the back seat, it . . . well, it wasn't in your head. It was real."

Rose Rita shuddered. "What . . . what was it?"

"I'd rather not say anything more right now," said Mrs. Zimmermann. "But I will tell you this. We've got to get home, and we've got to get home fast. I've got to get hold of my copy of the *Malleus Maleficarum*."

"The what?"

"The *Malleus Maleficarum*. It's a book that was written a long time ago by a monk. The title means The Hammer of Witches. That is, the book is a weapon to use in fighting off the attacks of those who fool around with black magic. It has a number of spells in it that will be of use to me. I should have memorized them long ago, but I didn't. So I need the book, and it's not the sort of thing you'd find at your friendly public library. We're going home the first thing in the morning, and I thought I ought to tell you why. I don't want to frighten you, but I figured you'd be frightened more if I went on being mysterious."

Rose Rita pointed at the strip of paper. "What're you gonna do with that?"

"Watch." Mrs. Zimmermann took a book of matches out of the drawer in the bedside table. She put the paper in an ashtray and lit it. While it burned, she made the sign of the cross over the ashtray and muttered a strange-sounding prayer. Rose Rita watched, fascinated. She felt scared, but she felt excited too, as if she had been suddenly swept out of her normal life and into an adventure.

That evening Rose Rita helped Mrs. Zimmermann pack. She got her own things together too. Mrs. Zimmermann informed her that Bessie was in the parking lot behind the hospital. A tow truck had pulled her up out of the juniper bushes, and the mechanics at a local garage had gone over her. She was all gassed and oiled and greased up, and ready to roll. A nurse came in with some papers for Mrs. Zimmermann to sign. The doctor paid one more visit, and said (rather coldly) that he hoped Mrs. Zimmermann had a good trip back. Everything was ready. Rose Rita and Mrs. Zimmermann crawled into bed and tried to get some sleep.

At first Rose Rita was too excited to sleep, but around midnight, she drifted off. Then, before she knew what was happening, she was awake again. Mrs. Zimmermann was standing by her bed. She was shaking her and shining a flashlight in her eyes.

"Come on, Rose Rita! Wake up!" Mrs. Zimmermann hissed. "We've got to go! Now!"

Rose Rita shook her head and rubbed her eyes. She fumbled for her glasses and put them on. "Wha . . . wha's the matter?"

"Wake up, I said! We're going to the farm. Now. We've got to!"

Rose Rita felt totally confused. "The *farm?* But I thought you said . . ."

"Never mind what I said. Get dressed and follow me. We're going back to the farm to . . . to get something I left there. Come on, you! Get a move on!" She shook Rose Rita again roughly, and flashed the light in her eyes. Rose Rita had never seen Mrs. Zimmermann act

this way before. Her voice was harsh, and her actions were rough and almost brutal. It was almost as if someone else had gotten inside of Mrs. Zimmermann's skin. And this business about going to the farm, instead of going straight home the way they had planned. What did it mean?

As Rose Rita dressed, Mrs. Zimmermann stood there, stiff and still, behind the white glaring halo of the flashlight. Rose Rita couldn't see her face, and she wasn't sure that she wanted to. When she was dressed, Rose Rita grabbed her valise and followed Mrs. Zimmermann. They tiptoed to the door, opened it a crack, and peered down the long dark hall. At the far end a nurse sat dozing behind a desk. An electric clock buzzed on the wall over her head. The whole hospital seemed to be asleep.

"Good!" said Mrs. Zimmermann, and she led the way down the hall to a set of stairs. The stairs led to the parking lot behind the hospital. There in the moonlight sat Bessie, the green Plymouth, staring patiently ahead as always. Rose Rita put the luggage in the trunk. Mrs. Zimmermann started the car, and they drove off.

It was a long hot dusty ride, all day, across the length of the Upper Peninsula. For Rose Rita, it was like a nightmare. Usually Mrs. Zimmermann was fun to travel with. She laughed and joked and sang songs, and talked a blue streak. When pestered, she even did little magic tricks, like snatching matches out of thin air, or throwing her voice into the weeds at the side of the road. But now, as they rode along, she was silent. She seemed to be brooding about something, but she wouldn't tell Rose Rita what it was. And Mrs. Zimmermann was nervous— very nervous. She glanced wildly from side to side, and sometimes got so jittery that she almost drove off the road. Rose Rita sat there rigid in her corner by the door, her sweaty hands at her sides. She didn't know what to do, or what to say.

The sun was going down over the Straits of Mackinac as Bessie chugged into the parking lot of the ferryboat landing at St. Ignace. A boat had just left, and Mrs. Zimmermann and Rose Rita had to wait a solid hour for the next one. They waited in silence, neither of them saying a word the whole time. Rose Rita went out and bought some sandwiches. It was her own idea—Mrs. Zimmermann had not stopped for lunch. Finally, though, the boat came in. It was called the *Grand Traverse Bay*. The sky was dark, and the moon was rising over the Straits, when Mrs. Zimmermann drove Bessie up the rattling gangplank and down into the black echoing hold of the ship.

When the car was parked, and the chocks had been placed under the wheels, Rose Rita started to get out, but then she discovered that Mrs. Zimmermann was just sitting there motionless behind the wheel.

"Mrs. Zimmermann?" Rose Rita called nervously. "Aren't you coming up?"

Mrs. Zimmermann gave a little start and shook her

head. She stared at Rose Rita as if she had never seen her before. "Come up? Oh . . . yes. Yes, of course. Be right with you." She got out of the car and, like a sleepwalker, clumped up the steps to the deck.

It ought to have been a very beautiful crossing. The moon shone down, silvering the decks and the ripply water of the Straits. Rose Rita tried to get Mrs. Zimmermann to walk around with her on the deck, but she wouldn't do it. She sat rigid on a bench and stared at her shoes. Rose Rita was frightened. This wasn't an adventure anymore. She wished, wished with all her heart, that they had never come on this trip. She wished they were back home in New Zebedee. Maybe if they were home, Uncle Jonathan, or Doc Humphries, or somebody, could figure out what was wrong with Mrs. Zimmermann and make her act like her old self again. Rose Rita didn't feel as if she could do anything for Mrs. Zimmermann. She felt utterly helpless. All she could do was tag along. Tag along, and wait.

An hour or so later Mrs. Zimmermann and Rose Rita were driving down the gravel road that led to Oley Gunderson's farm. They passed Gert Bigger's store and saw that it was closed. A tiny night light burned on the porch.

Rose Rita couldn't stand it any longer. "Mrs. Zimmermann," she burst out. "Why are we going to the farm? What's this all about?"

At first Mrs. Zimmermann was silent. Then she said,

in a slow dull voice, "I don't know why. There's something I have to do there, but I can't remember what it is."

They drove on. Gravel crackled and popped under the car's tires, and sometimes long leafy branches whipped across the doors or the roof. Now it began to rain. Big drops started to splat on the windshield, and Rose Rita heard the dull rolling of thunder. Flashes of lightning leaped out in front of the car. Now they were at the farm. As they drove into the yard, a bright flash lit up the front of the barn, showing the two staring window-eyes, and the yawning mouth of the door. It was like a monster mouth, opening to swallow them up.

Because it was raining outside, Rose Rita and Mrs. Zimmermann went into the house by way of the long covered walkway that ran from the house to the barn. But when they unlocked the door and tried to turn the lights on, nothing happened. Mrs. Zimmermann had forgotten to pay Oley's overdue electric bill, and the current had been shut off since their first visit. After digging around in a cupboard, Mrs. Zimmermann found a kerosene lamp. She lit it and put it on the kitchen table. Rose Rita opened up the picnic hamper, and they sat down to eat the sandwiches Rose Rita had bought. They ate in silence. In the smoky yellow light Mrs. Zimmermann's face looked haggard and worn. She also looked tense, very tense, as if she was waiting for something to happen. Rose Rita looked nervously over her shoulder. Beyond the circle of friendly lamplight the house lay in shadow. The staircase was a well of darkness. Rose Rita realized, with a sudden sick feeling, that she would have to go up those stairs to bed. She didn't want to go to bed. She didn't want to stay in Oley's house for another minute. She wanted to bundle Mrs. Zimmermann into the car and make her drive them back to New Zebedee, even if they had to drive all night. But Rose Rita didn't say anything. She made no move. Whatever the spell was that lay over Mrs. Zimmermann, it lay over Rose Rita too. She felt utterly totally powerless.

Outside it was pouring. There was a tin roof on the front porch, and the sound of the rain hitting it was a steady drumming roar. Finally, with an effort, Rose Rita pushed back her chair. She stood up.

"I think we . . . we oughta go to bed, Mrs. Zimmermann," she said hoarsely. Her voice was faint and seemed to be coming from deep down inside her.

"You go on, Rose Rita. I want to sit here and . . . and think a bit." Mrs. Zimmermann's voice was wooden and mechanical, and unbelievably weary. It almost sounded as if she were talking in her sleep.

Rose Rita backed away fearfully. She picked up her valise, took out her flashlight, and turned toward the stairs. As Rose Rita went up the steps, flashlight in hand, her shadow and the shadow of the railing danced weirdly on the wall next to her. Halfway up Rose Rita stopped and looked down. There sat Mrs. Zimmermann in the circle of yellow lamplight. Her hands were folded on the table, and she was staring straight ahead of her. Rose Rita had the feeling that, if she called to her, she wouldn't get any answer. She swallowed hard and went on up the stairs.

The bedroom with the black walnut bed was just as Rose Rita had left it. She began to peel back the spread, but halfway she stopped. She stopped because she had heard a noise from downstairs. A single small noise. Tap. The sound of Mrs. Zimmermann's ring. Now the sound was repeated, three times over. Tap . . . tap . . . tap. The sound was slow and mechanical, like the ticking of a big clock. Rose Rita stood there, flashlight in hand. She listened to the sound and wondered what it meant.

Suddenly a door slammed.

Rose Rita gave a little yelp and spun around. She dashed out of the room and down the stairs. On the landing she froze. There was the table, with the lamp burning on it. There was Mrs. Zimmermann's purse, and her cigar case. The front door was open. It banged gently in the wind. Mrs. Zimmermann was gone.

CHAPTER SEVEN

Rose Rita stood on the front porch of the farmhouse. Her flashlight dangled from one hand and made a pool of light at her feet. Slashes of rain cut across her shoes, and lightning lit up the wildly thrashing trees across the road. Thunder rolled. Rose Rita felt stunned. She felt as if she were walking in her sleep. Mrs. Zimmermann was gone. But where had she gone, and why? What had happened to her?

Cupping her hands to her mouth, Rose Rita called, "Mrs. Zimmermann! Mrs. Zimmermann!" but she got no answer. Slowly she picked her way down the steps, waving the flashlight in front of her. At the bottom of the steps she stopped and looked around. If Mrs. Zimmermann had run out the front door and down the front steps, it ought to have been easy to tell which way she went after that. The front yard was full of long grass, and Rose Rita and Mrs. Zimmermann had not touched it on the night before, because they had come into the house by using the covered walkway. Now, as Rose Rita moved her flashlight around, she saw a little patch of grass trampled down at the bottom of the steps. But no path led away, in any direction. The grass grew all around, tall and shiny and untouched. It was as if Mrs. Zimmermann had evaporated.

Panic seized Rose Rita. Yelling "Mrs. Zimmermann!" at the top of her voice, she thrashed through the wet grass till she came to the road. She looked to the right. She looked to the left. Nothing but darkness and rain. Rose Rita fell to her knees in a puddle and started to cry. She covered her face with her hands and sobbed bitterly. The cold rain poured down on her and soaked her to the skin.

At long last she got up. Staggering like a drunken person, half blinded by tears, she made her way back to the farmhouse. But on the front porch she stopped. She did not want to go back into that house. Not now, in the dark. With a shudder Rose Rita turned away. But where could she go?

Bessie. She thought of Bessie sitting in the barn. The barn was a dark spooky place, like the house, but Bessie was a friendly creature. Rose Rita really thought of the car as a living breathing person now. She could go and sleep in the car. It wouldn't hurt her—it would protect her. Rose Rita took a deep shuddering breath, clenched her fists, and started walking toward the barn. Rain slashed across her as she went.

The sound of the big white door rolling back echoed in the high raftered ceiling of the barn. There was Bessie, waiting. Rose Rita patted her hood and climbed into the back seat. She locked all the doors. Then she lay down and tried to sleep, but it was no use. She was too tense. All night Rose Rita lay there, wet and frightened and tired and alone. Once or twice she sat up suddenly when she thought she saw a face at the window of the car. But it was all her imagination—there was no one there.

As she lay staring at the ceiling of the car and listening to the storm, Rose Rita thought. Mrs. Zimmermann had disappeared. Disappeared as if by magic. In fact, there was no "as if" about it. Mrs. Zimmermann's disappearance had been caused by magic.

Rose Rita went over the sequence of events in her mind: first there had been Oley's weird letter about a magic ring, and then the empty ring box. Then came the mutilated photograph, and the shadow Rose Rita had seen moving around in Mrs. Zimmermann's bedroom that night. Then those horrible pains, and the slip of paper, and the strange way Mrs. Zimmermann had behaved on the trip back to the farm. But what was the key to the whole thing? Was the ring the key? Did somebody have it, and had they used it to do things to Mrs. Zimmermann? That seemed like a reasonable explanation to Rose Rita. But a heck of a lot of good reasonable explanations were going to do her. Mrs. Zimmermann was gone, and Rose Rita didn't know where to go to find her. Maybe she was dead. And as for the magic ring, if there was such a thing . . . well, Rose Rita didn't know who had it, and she hadn't the faintest idea of what she would do if she *did* know. So there she was.

Rose Rita thought like this, in endless circles, all the night long, while thunder rolled overhead and lightning lit up, now and then, the high dusty windows of the barn. Finally morning came. Rose Rita stumbled out into the sunlight to find everything looking sparkling and fresh and green. Blackbirds were gorging themselves on the mulberries in a crooked old tree in the front yard. Rose Rita felt a sudden burst of cheerfulness, but then she remembered Mrs. Zimmermann, and she burst into tears again. No, she said firmly to herself, blinking back her tears and brushing hair out of her eyes. You're not going to cry. That's not any good, you dumb dope. You've got to *do* something!

But what was she going to do? Here she was, alone, three hundred miles from home. For one wild instant she thought that she might drive Bessie all the way back to New Zebedee. After all she had driven the car for a little way, on that back road near Ironwood. But Rose Rita was scared. Scared of getting picked up by a policeman, scared of having an accident. Besides, driving home wouldn't help find Mrs. Zimmermann. She had to think of something else.

Rose Rita sat down on the front steps, put her head in her hands, and thought some more. Should she call up her folks and have them come and get her? She could hear what her father would say: "You see, Louise, that's what happens when you let Rose Rita run around with screwballs! The old bat flew off on a broom and left Rose Rita there to rot. Well, maybe the next time you think of letting our daughter go tooting off with a screwball you'll . . ." Rose Rita winced. She didn't want to face her father, not without Mrs. Zimmermann. Rose Rita thought some more.

Rose Rita racked her brains. She crossed and recrossed her legs and bit her lip and fumed. She was a real fighter, and she wasn't going to abandon Mrs. Zimmermann. Not if there was something she could do.

Rose Rita jumped up and snapped her fingers. Of course! What a dope she had been! Why hadn't she thought of this before? There was that book, that Mallet of Something, or whatever it was called. The book that Mrs. Zimmermann had been going home to get when she changed her mind—or somebody changed it for her. But Rose Rita didn't have the book. She didn't even know where she could get a copy. She sat down again.

Rose Rita thought about magic books for a while.

Rows of them, standing on shelves, books with spotted vellum covers and curly writing on their spines. *That was it!* Jonathan had magic books. He had a whole big collection of them. And what was more, he had the key to Mrs. Zimmermann's house. If he couldn't find that old Mallet Whatchmacallit, he could just go next door and dig it out of Mrs. Zimmermann's bookcase. Also, Jonathan knew about magic, because he was a wizard himself. Rose Rita could tell him what had happened, and he wouldn't think she had gone off her rocker. Good old Jonathan! He would know what to do.

Rose Rita got up and went into the house. There was an old-fashioned crank phone on the wall in the kitchen. Rose Rita took the receiver off the hook and gave the crank a few twirls. The bell inside the box rang, but the line was dead. Mrs. Zimmermann had forgotten to pay Oley's electric bill, and she had also forgotten to pay the phone bill.

Rose Rita hung up the receiver and stood there, feeling depressed. But then she remembered Gert Bigger's store. There was probably a phone there she could use. Rose Rita didn't want to have anything more to do with the crabby old woman who had cheated Mrs. Zimmermann that night they ran out of gas, but she didn't see any way around it. Gert Bigger's store was only a couple of miles down the road. Rose Rita sighed. She would just have to walk there and get help.

Rose Rita started out. It was already a hot day, even

though it was early in the morning, and the road was dusty. Steam rose from Rose Rita's clothing, which was still wet from the night before. She wondered if she would catch cold, but she didn't wonder very hard. Catching cold was the least of her worries right now.

It was farther to Gert Bigger's store than Rose Rita had thought it would be. Flies were buzzing around when Rose Rita rounded a bend and saw the store shimmering there in the heat. It looked pretty much the way it had when she saw it the first time. But as she got closer to the store, Rose Rita noticed one difference. There was a chicken in the chicken yard. Just one. A bedraggled-looking white hen. As soon as the chicken saw Rose Rita, it began to cluck excitedly and run back and forth. Rose Rita smiled. She had had a white hen for a pet once. It was called Henny Penny. This poor lonely chicken reminded her of it. Rose Rita wondered why the chicken was so excited, and then she noticed a stump in one corner of the yard. There was an ax leaning against it. It looked as if old Henry Penny was going into the pot before long. Poor thing, Rose Rita thought. It probably thinks I'm coming to chop off its head.

Rose Rita turned away and started up the steps to the store, but as she did so, she almost stepped on a small black dog. It was the same dog that had barked at her and Mrs. Zimmermann that other time. It must have been hunched down on the steps in the shadow, because Rose Rita could have sworn that the steps were empty when she glanced at them a second before. Imitating Mrs. Zimmermann, Rose Rita pulled back her foot as if she were going to kick the dog, and, as before, the dog ran off into the shubbery and disappeared.

Rose Rita walked up the steps. She opened the door and looked in. There was Gert Bigger, kneeling in the middle of the floor. She was unpacking cereal boxes and stacking them on a shelf.

"Well," she said, glaring at Rose Rita. "What do *you* want?"

"I . . . I have to make a phone call," said Rose Rita. Her voice was trembling as she spoke, and she was afraid she was going to burst into tears.

"You do, huh? Well, you better have some money handy. There's a pay phone over there on that wall." Gert Bigger pointed towards a scarred black phone at the end of the counter.

Rose Rita dug into her pocket and came up with a dime and a couple of pennies. She would have to make it a collect call.

As she walked down the aisle toward the phone, Rose Rita was aware that Gert Bigger was watching her. She wondered why. Oh, well, thought Rose Rita, she's just nosy. She dumped her coins on a little shelf in front of the phone and read the yellow sheet of instructions. For a collect call, she would have to dial O for the operator. Rose Rita put her finger in the O-hole and was just starting to dial, when she saw, out of the corner of her eye, that Gert Bigger was still staring at her. She had let her work go and was just kneeling there in the middle of the aisle, watching.

Rose Rita stopped in mid-dial. She took her finger out and let the little wheel click back into place. She had just had a very strange thought: What if Gert Bigger had done something to Mrs. Zimmermann? She had a grudge against Mrs. Zimmermann—Rose Rita knew that. And she lived close to Oley's farm. She might've broken in to steal that magic ring after he died. It was a crazy notion, and Rose Rita knew it was crazy. But she still wondered if she might be onto something.

She turned, and her gaze met Gert Bigger's.

"What's the matter now?" Gert Bigger growled. "You forget the number you were supposed to call?"

"Uh . . . yeah, I mean, no ma'am, er . . . never mind," Rose Rita stammered. She turned to the phone. This is dumb, she told herself. That crabby old lady isn't any witch. She doesn't have any magic ring. Just stop playing detective and make your crummy phone call and get it over with!

Rose Rita dialed O and got the operator. She told her that she wanted to make a collect call to New Zebedee, Michigan, to Mr. Jonathan Barnavelt. His number was 865. Rose Rita waited. She heard vague scratchy and fumbly sounds, and then she heard the buzzing sound that meant that the operator was ringing Jonathan's phone. *Bzz. Bzz. Bzz.*

"I beg your pardon," said the operator, "but the party does not answer. Would you—"

"Please try a little longer," said Rose Rita. "Please, ma'am. It's an emergency."

"Very well." The ringing went on.

As she waited, Rose Rita's eyes began to wander. On the wall next to the phone she saw an old photograph in a black frame. It was a picture of a man in an old-fashioned suit. He had a handlebar mustache . . .

Rose Rita froze. She knew who the man was. He was the man in the picture Mrs. Zimmermann had found in the junk shop. And now she remembered his name: Mordecai. Mordecai Hunks. He was the man Mrs. Zimmermann and Gert Bigger had fought over, a long time ago. He was the reason for Gert Bigger's hatred of Mrs. Zimmermann, her long-standing grudge. It was all beginning to fall together now . . .

Rose Rita turned her head slightly and glanced toward Mrs. Bigger. But at that moment a horn beeped outside. Somebody wanted gas. Gert Bigger heaved a discontented sigh, got up heavily, and stumped to the door.

"I'm sorry, Miss," said the operator, "but I cannot continue to ring the party's number. Would you care to call back at another time?"

Rose Rita was startled. She had forgotten about the phone call she was making. "Uh . . . okay," she mumbled. "I'll . . . uh, try later. Thanks."

Rose Rita hung up the phone and glanced quickly

around. Now was her chance. Behind the counter was a doorway covered by a heavy brown curtain. Rose Rita looked again toward the front of the store. Through the wide plate glass window, she could see Gert Bigger pumping gas. And now she saw another car pulling up on the other side of the pumps. The old bat would probably be out there for a while. Rose Rita took a deep breath, pulled the curtain aside, and ducked in through the doorway.

She found herself in an ugly little room with pale green walls. There was a coal company calendar on the wall and a bare bulb dangling from the ceiling. A small iron safe stood in one corner, and against the long wall was a high narrow shelflike desk. On the desk was a faded green blotter with columns of figures added up all over it. Arranged neatly next to the blotter were a bottle of Parker's Quink, a pile of wooden pens with rusty metal nibs, a brown gum eraser, and several well-sharpened pencils. On the other side of the blotter was an account book with a green cardboard cover. The date 1950 was printed on the cover. There was nothing here that looked in any way magical.

Rose Rita's heart sank. She felt foolish for doing what she was doing. But wait a minute. What were these? Rose Rita knelt down. Under the desk was a shelf, and on it were piled more green-covered account books. They looked just like the one on the desk, except that they were very dusty and had different dates. 1949,

1948, and so on back. Rose Rita opened one up. Just dull columns of figures. Debits, credits, receipts, and stuff like that. She was about to put the book back when she noticed something sticking out of the middle. She pulled it out and found that it was a folded piece of paper. When she opened the paper, she found a drawing done in pencil. It looked like this:

Rose Rita held the paper with trembling hands. She could feel her heart beating faster. She was no wizard, but she knew what this was, because she had once been allowed a closely supervised look into one of Uncle Jonathan's magic books. The drawing was a magic pentacle, one of those charms that witches and wizards use when they want good things or bad things to happen. Rose Rita stared at the drawing. She stared at it so long and so hard that she did not hear the soft tinkle of the bell as the front door of the store was quietly opened and carefully closed. A board creaked behind her. Suddenly the curtain was whipped aside, and Rose Rita turned to find Gert Bigger standing over her.

"Well now! What do you think you're doin'? Eh?"

CHAPTER EIGHT

Rose Rita knelt there on the floor and looked up at Gert Bigger's angry face. In her trembling hands she still held the piece of paper with the strange drawing on it.

Gert Bigger stepped into the little room and pulled the curtain shut behind her. "I asked you, Miss, what you think you're doing? There's a law against trespassing, you know, and there are reform schools for girls who steal things. Would you like your parents to know what you've been up to? Eh? Would you?"

Rose Rita opened her mouth to speak, but all that came out was "I . . . I . . . please . . . I didn't mean . . ."

Gert Bigger took a step forward. She reached down and snatched the paper from Rose Rita's numb fingers.

Silence fell while Gert Bigger stood there looking from the paper to Rose Rita and back to the paper again. She seemed to be trying to make up her mind.

At that moment the bell on the front door of the store jangled, and a voice yelled "Yoo-hoo, Gertie! Are you home?"

Gert Bigger turned and swore under her breath. Rose Rita jumped up and ducked out through the narrow curtained opening. She sprinted down the main aisle of the store, right past the surprised face of a middle-aged woman with a shopping bag in her hand. Slam went the door behind her. Rose Rita clattered down the steps and dashed across the road. She ran blindly, and she could hear herself crying as she ran. She cut across the corner of a cornfield, trampling the wrinkly green plants underfoot. Her feet found a pathway of green grass that ran along the edge of the cornfield and up over the top of a low hill. Rose Rita ran up it, ran as hard as she could, until she collapsed under a droopy elm tree that grew near a flat-topped boulder. She threw herself down on the grass, tore off her glasses, and cried.

Rose Rita lay there crying for a long time. She was tired and hungry and frightened and alone. She hadn't had any food at all since last night, and she had gotten almost no sleep. At first she was afraid that Gert Bigger would come after her. At any moment her hand would be on Rose Rita's shoulder. But Gert Bigger never came. Rose Rita went on crying, but she could feel her body

starting to relax. She didn't care about anything now . . . anything at all. It was a delicious feeling. Slowly her mind started to drift off. It was so nice lying here in the shade . . . so very, very nice . . . but it would be even nicer to be home. Home . . . in . . .

Rose Rita's eyes closed. A soft breeze rustled through the corn, and in the distance a fly was lazily buzzing. Rose Rita shook her head, fighting weakly against the drowsiness that was falling over her. She was trying to think of something. What was it? She never found out, because in a very few minutes she was fast asleep.

"Hey you, wake up! You better wake up! Don't you know it's bad to sleep on the wet ground? You might catch cold. Come on, wake up."

Rose Rita awoke to hear this worried insistent voice speaking to her. She shook her head and looked up. All she saw was a blur. Then she remembered her glasses. After fumbling a bit in the grass near her, she located them and put them on. When she looked up, Rose Rita saw a girl about her own age. She was wearing a short-sleeved plaid shirt and jeans, and muddy army boots. The girl had straight dishwater-blonde hair, and it was combed down on both sides of her head. Her face was longish, and it had a sad worried expression. The dark eyebrows curved up into worry lines. Rose Rita thought that she had seen this face somewhere before. But where?

When she remembered, she almost laughed. The girl looked just like the Jack of Clubs.

"Hi there," said the girl. "Gee, I'm glad you woke up! Didn't anybody ever tell you it was bad to sleep on the ground when it's wet? It rained last night, you know."

"Yeah, I know," said Rose Rita. She got up and put out her hand. "I'm Rose Rita Pottinger. What's your name?"

"Agatha Sipes. They call me Aggie for short. I live up that way, over that hill. This's my father's farm. By the way, are you the one that stomped all over those corn plants back there?"

Rose Rita nodded sadly. "Yeah, that was me. I'm sorry, but I was crying so hard that I didn't look where I was going."

The girl looked worried. "You oughtn't to do that kind of thing. Farmers work hard for their living." She added, in a less severe tone, "Why were you crying?"

Rose Rita opened her mouth, but then she hesitated. She wanted to tell her troubles to someone, but she wanted to be believed. "My friend Mrs. Zimmermann is lost, and I don't know where to find her. We were staying at a farm down the road last night, and she ran out the front door and just disappeared."

The girl rubbed her chin and looked wise. "Oh, I'll bet I know what happened. She probably went walkin' in the woods and got lost. It happens to lots of people up here in the summertime. Let's go up to my place, and we'll call up the sheriff's department, and they'll send out some people to look for her. They'll find her all right."

Rose Rita thought of the circle of trampled grass in front of the farmhouse. The circle with no path leading away. It was no use. She'd just have to tell the truth and risk the consequences. "Do . . . do you believe in magic?" she said suddenly.

The girl looked startled. "Huh?"

"I said, do you believe in magic?"

"You mean ghosts and witches and magic spells and stuff like that?"

"Yeah."

Agatha grinned shyly. "Yeah, I do. I know you're not supposed to, but I can't help it." She added, in a worried voice, "Sometimes I think there's a ghost in the cellar in our house, but Mom says it's just the wind at night. You don't think there's a ghost in our cellar, do you?"

"How would I know?" said Rose Rita, in an irritated voice. "Hey, do you want to hear about what happened to Mrs. Zimmermann or don't you?"

"Sure I want to hear. I really do. Tell me all about it."

Rose Rita and Agatha Sipes sat down on the grass under the elm tree. Rose Rita's stomach growled, and she remembered that she hadn't eaten since last night. She was terribly hungry. But she wanted to tell her story, and Agatha seemed eager to listen. Rose Rita began.

She told the whole story, as far as she knew it, from Oley's mysterious letter and the empty ring box, on through the very strange things that had been happening to her and Mrs. Zimmermann lately. When she got to the part about Mrs. Zimmermann's disappearance, Agatha's eyes grew wide. And when she described her run-in with Mrs. Bigger, Agatha's eyes got even wider, and her mouth dropped open. She glanced nervously in the direction of Gert Bigger's store.

"My gosh!" she said. "It's a wonder she didn't kill you! And you know what? I bet she's the one who made your friend disappear."

Rose Rita looked strangely at Agatha. "Do . . . do you know anything about her? Mrs. Bigger, I mean?"

"I sure do. She's a witch."

Now it was Rose Rita's turn to be flabbergasted. "Huh? How do you know?"

"How do I know? Because last year I worked in the Ellis Corners library, and she came in and took out every last book about magic that we had, that's how I know. Some of 'em were in the Reference Room, and she couldn't take 'em out, so she just sat there for hours and read. I asked Mrs. Bryer the librarian about her, and she said Mrs. Bigger had been doing that for years. Said she had library cards for all the libraries around here, and took out all the magic books she could find. Mrs. Bryer says she reads the covers off of 'em and never takes 'em back till the library starts houndin' her. Isn't that weird?"

"Yeah, it sure is." Rose Rita felt strange. She was wildly elated, because her hunch had been proved right —at least, she felt that it had been proved right. But at the same time she felt helpless and scared. If Mrs. Bigger really was a witch, what could she and Aggie do about it?

Rose Rita got up and paced around. Then she sat down on the flat-topped boulder and lapsed into deep thought. Aggie stood near her, looking uncomfortable. She shifted nervously from one foot to the other, and puckered up her eyebrows into the most worried frown she had produced yet. "Did I say something wrong, Rose Rita?" she asked, after several silent minutes had passed. "If I did, I'm sorry, I really am."

Rose Rita shook herself out of her trance and looked up. "No, Aggie, you didn't say anything wrong. Honest you didn't. But I just don't know what to do. If you're right, and old Mrs. Bigger is a witch, and she has done something to Mrs. Zimmermann, then . . . well, what can we do? Just the two of us, I mean."

"I don't know."

"Neither do I."

More silence. Silence for a good five minutes. Then Aggie spoke up again.

"Hey, I know what let's do. Let's go home to my house and have some lunch. My mom always fixes a lot of food, because we have a really big family, and I'm sure there'd be enough for you. Come on. After lunch maybe we can figure out what to do. You can't think good on an empty stomach. That's what my dad says, anyway."

Rose Rita looked reluctant, but she really didn't have any better ideas. On the way to the farmhouse Aggie talked a blue streak. She talked about things that she was worried about, like rabies and tetanus and electrical shock and mayonnaise that has been left out of the icebox too long. Rose Rita, however, was only half listening. She was still thinking, trying to make up her mind what to do. Should she give up playing Nancy Drew, girl detective, and call her folks and have them come and get her? No. Rose Rita was a stubborn girl, and she still thought she might be able to find Mrs. Zimmermann without the aid of her parents. What Aggie had told her about Mrs. Bigger and the magic books had made her more certain than ever that Mrs. Zimmermann had been carried off by witchcraft of some kind. So Rose Rita went back to her idea of calling Jonathan. She would do that as soon as she got to Aggie's house. With her mind racing along in high gear, Rose Rita tried to figure out what her next move would be. What should she say to Mrs. Sipes about what had happened?

They were within sight of the farmhouse when Rose Rita reached out and grabbed Aggie's arm. "Wait a minute, Aggie."

"Why? What's the matter?"

"We have to think up a story to tell your mother. I

can't tell her what I told you. She'll think I'm crazy. I can't even tell her my real name, because then she'd want to call up my folks, and I don't want her to call them up."

Aggie frowned. "I don't think you ought to lie to my mother. It's not nice to lie, and anyway I think you'll get caught. My mom is pretty smart. She'd see through it in a minute."

When people disagreed with Rose Rita, it usually made her mad. But in this case she was doubly mad, because she was proud of her ability to make up alibis and excuses. Making up excuses is hard, and it is not quite the same thing as telling tall stories. You have to be able to come up with a story that people will believe. And Rose Rita could really do that—most of the time.

Rose Rita threw an irritated glance at Aggie. "Your mom isn't the smartest person in the world, I bet. And anyway, I'm good at making things up. All we have to do is sit down and figure out a story. Then we both memorize it, so there won't be any slip-ups."

Now it was Aggie's turn to be crabby. "Oh yeah? What're we gonna tell her? Here's my new friend, Rose Rita, who just fell out of a flying saucer?"

"No, dope. We don't tell her something like that. We tell her something she'll think is true. And then we call Uncle Jonathan and get him to tell us what kind of spell to say to make Mrs. Bigger tell us what she did with Mrs. Zimmermann. Okay?"

Aggie bit her lip and wrinkled up her forehead. She took a deep breath and let it out. "Oh all right. But if we get caught, I'm gonna say it's all your fault. I'm not gonna get bawled out just because you think it's nice to lie to people."

Rose Rita gritted her teeth. "I don't think it's nice to lie. But we have to, that's all. Now come on. This is what we'll say . . ."

A bell began to ring. A little sharp clangy handbell was calling people in for lunch at the Sipes farmhouse. Aggie started forward, but Rose Rita grabbed her arm and dragged her over behind a forsythia bush. She put her lips to Aggie's ear and started to whisper.

CHAPTER NINE

The Sipes farmhouse was big and white, with a wide screened-in porch. Spirea bushes grew next to the porch, and there were peony bushes in the front yard. A large apple tree grew on one side of the house, and from one of its saggy limbs hung a tractor tire on a rope. There were kids' things scattered all over the yard. Baseball bats, bicycles, tricycles, puzzles, dolls, toy trucks, and plastic machine guns. Things like that. But when Aggie opened the front door, Rose Rita was struck by how neat and clean the house was inside. All the woodwork shone with polish, and there were doilies or embroidered runners on all the tables, chests, and shelves. There was a flowered carpet on the staircase, and a shelf clock ticking in the front hall. A pleasant smell of cooking was in the air.

Aggie took Rose Rita straight out to the kitchen and introduced her to her mother. Mrs. Sipes had the same long face and worry eyebrows that her daughter had, but she seemed friendly enough. She wiped her floury hands on her apron and greeted Rose Rita warmly.

"Hi! Glad to meet you! I wondered what was keeping Aggie. I rang the bell for lunch about five times, and I had just about given up on her. What did you say your name was?"

Rose Rita hesitated, just a second. "Uh, Rosemary. Rosemary Potts."

"What a nice name! Hi, Rosemary! How're you? Are you visiting in the neighborhood? I don't think I've seen you around before."

Rose Rita squirmed uncomfortably. "Uh, no, you haven't on . . . on account of I was just up here on vacation with . . . with Mrs. Zimmermann." Rose Rita paused. "She's a friend of my family, a real good friend," she added quickly.

"Yeah," Aggie added. "Mrs. Whatsername and Rose . . . uh, Rosemary's family are real good friends, they really are. Only Mrs. . . . Mrs. . . . ."

"Zimmermann," said Rose Rita, giving Aggie a dirty look.

"Oh, yeah. Mrs. Zimmermann. Well, old Oley—you

know him, Ma—he left Mrs. Zimmermann his farm, and she and Rosemary came up to look at it, and last night Mrs. Zimmermann wandered off into the woods out behind the farm, and she disappeared."

"Yeah," said Rose Rita. "I think she must've gotten lost. Anyway, I can't find her anywhere, and I'm getting scared."

Rose Rita held her breath. Would Mrs. Sipes believe this tale?

"Oh, Rosemary!" exclaimed Mrs. Sipes, putting her arm around her. "What an awful thing to happen! Look, I tell you what I'll do. I'll get on the phone and call up the sheriff's office and they'll get some of their men out there, right away quick, to search for her. There was someone who got lost in the woods up here only last year, and they found him before he got hurt. So don't worry. Your friend'll be all right."

Inwardly Rose Rita breathed a sigh of relief. She hated to lie about Mrs. Zimmermann's disappearance, and she was (in reality) worried sick about her. But she just didn't know what Mrs. Sipes would say if she were to tell her that Mrs. Zimmermann had disappeared right into thin air.

Later, after the call to the sheriff's department had been made, Rose Rita was sitting at a long dining room table with Aggie and seven other children and Mrs. Sipes. Rose Rita was sitting at the head of the table, in the place where Mr. Sipes usually sat. Mr. Sipes was away overnight in Petoskey, on business.

Rose Rita looked around the table. It was a worried-looking family. They all had those long faces and up-turned eyebrows. There were tall kids and short kids, five boys and two girls (counting Aggie) and a baby in a highchair. On the table was a big platter of corned beef, potatoes, onions, and carrots, and there were more vegetables and some dumplings in the two smoking dishes that stood nearby. There was a cutting board with freshly baked bread on it, and there were two big pitchers of milk. Mrs. Sipes said grace, and then everybody dug in.

"Let Rosemary have some first," said Mrs. Sipes. "She's our guest, you know."

It took Rose Rita a second to recognize her new name. In fact she was startled when someone shoved a tureen of mashed carrots at her. "Oh . . . uh, thanks," she mumbled, and she helped herself to some.

Later on, when everyone had been served, Mrs. Sipes said in a loud clear voice, "Children, I think you should know that Rosemary here has had an accident. The friend she was traveling with got lost in the forest, and we're trying to find her. We've sent the sheriff's patrol out to look for her."

"I think anybody who gets lost in the woods over here must really be dumb," said a tall boy with black curly hair.

"Leonard!" said Mrs. Sipes in a shocked voice. "That will be *quite* enough out of you!" She turned to Rose Rita and smiled sympathetically. "I must apologize for my rude son. Tell us, Rosemary, where do you come from?"

"New Zebedee, ma'am. It's a little town way down near the bottom of the state. Probably you never heard of it."

"I think I know where it is," said Mrs. Sipes. "Now then. I really think we'd better notify your parents. They'll want to know what's happened. What is your father's name?"

Rose Rita stared at the tablecloth. She stuck out her lower lip and looked as sad as she could. "My folks are dead. Both of them. I live with my uncle Jonathan. He's my legal guardian, and his name is Jonathan Barnavelt, and he lives at 100 High Street."

Mrs. Sipes looked surprised and saddened. "My lord, you poor girl! What a string of misfortunes! First your parents dead, and now this to happen to you! Tell me, my dear. How did it happen?"

Rose Rita blinked. "How did what happen?"

"How did your parents happen to die? Excuse me for going into something so sad right at this present moment, but I couldn't help wondering what had happened to them."

Rose Rita paused. There was a mischievous gleam in her eye. She was beginning to enjoy her own lying. At first she had been afraid of being found out, but now that Mrs. Sipes had swallowed both the lost-in-the-forest story and the orphan story—not to mention Rose Rita's fake name—Rose Rita began to think that she would swallow anything. And inwardly she was chortling at her own cleverness in having made up the part about Jonathan being her guardian. There was a good one, since it would allow her to call up Jonathan and find out what she wanted to know, without any more fooling around. Rose Rita had intended to just say that her folks had been killed in a car accident, but now she decided to try for something fancy. It wouldn't do any harm.

"My folks got killed in a funny kind of way," she began. "You see, my dad used to be a forest ranger. He used to walk around in the woods a lot and make sure there weren't any forest fires, and that kind of thing. Well, one day he came across this beaver dam, and it was a really weird-looking kind of dam—all messy and screwed up. My dad had never seen a beaver dam that looked like it, not ever, and he wondered how come it looked the way it did. You see, what he didn't know was, the dam had been built by a beaver that had rabies. And then my dad brought my mom out to look at the dam, and the beaver bit 'em both, and they died."

Silence. Dead silence. Then Aggie's sister tittered, and one of the boys laughed.

"Gee," said Leonard in a loud sarcastic voice, "I

would've thought that if a beaver had the rabies, he would just run off into the woods and die. Wouldn't you think so, Ted?"

"Yeah," said the boy who was sitting next to Leonard. "I never heard of anyone gettin' bit by a beaver that had rabies. And anyway, if that's what really happened, how'd you ever find out? If your folks got bit and died, they wouldn't of told you nothin', would they?"

Rose Rita could feel her face getting red. Everyone was looking at her, and she felt as if she were sitting there without any clothes on. She stared hard at her plate and mumbled, "It was a real rare kind of rabies."

More silence. More staring. Finally Mrs. Sipes cleared her throat and said, "Uh, Rosemary, I think you'd better come into the other room with me for a minute, if you don't mind. And Aggie, you'd better come too."

Aggie got up and followed Rose Rita out of the room. With Mrs. Sipes leading the way, the glum little procession wound its way up the stairs and into a bedroom at the front of the house. Rose Rita and Aggie sat down side by side on the bed, and Mrs. Sipes closed the door softly behind her.

"Now then," she said, folding her arms and staring hard at Rose Rita. "I have heard incredible stories in my time, but this one just about takes the cake. I thought there was something odd about that orphan tale, but— Rosemary . . . by the way, is that your real name?"

Rose Rita shook her head. "No, ma'am," she said, in a tearful voice. "It's Rose Rita."

Mrs. Sipes smiled a faint little smile. "Well, at least it's fairly similar. Now listen, Rose Rita," she said, staring straight into her eyes, "if you're in some kind of trouble, I'd like to help you. I don't know what moved you to concoct that ridiculous story about the beaver, but you'll have to lie better than that if you want to grow up to be a con man, or a con girl, or whatever it is you want to be. Now do you suppose you could tell me, honestly and truly, what happened and why you're here?"

Rose Rita glared balefully at Mrs. Sipes. She wondered what Mrs. Sipes would say if she told her about the patch of trampled grass with no path leading away from it. "I told you, Mrs. Sipes," said Rose Rita stubbornly, "I told you that my friend Mrs. Zimmermann is lost, and I don't know where she is. Honest to God."

Mrs. Sipes sighed. "Well, my dear, I suppose *that* part of your story may be true. But I have never heard such an atrocious lie as that beaver story, really I haven't! Bit by a rabid beaver, indeed! And now you tell me that your real name is Rose Rita. All right, let's have some more of the truth. Are your parents dead, or alive?"

"My folks are alive," said Rose Rita, in a dull hopeless voice. "And their names are George and Louise Pottinger, and they live at 39 Mansion Street in New Zebedee, Michigan. And I'm their daughter. I really am. Honest. Cross my heart and hope to die."

Mrs. Sipes smiled sympathetically at Rose Rita. "There now. Isn't it easier to tell the truth?"

Not much, thought Rose Rita, but she said nothing.

Mrs. Sipes sighed again and shook her head. "I don't understand you, Rose Rita. I honestly don't. If it's true that you were traveling with a friend of your family's named Mrs. Zimmermann—"

"It's true, all right," said Rose Rita, interrupting. "Her handbag is still on the kitchen table in that crummy old farmhouse, and it's probably got her driver's license and a lot of other stuff in it with her name on it. So there." She folded her arms and glared fiercely at Mrs. Sipes.

"Very well," said Mrs. Sipes calmly. "As I was saying, if that part of your story is true, why on earth did you try to hide your parents' identity?"

An answer sprang into Rose Rita's head, an answer that was partly true. "On account of my dad doesn't like Mrs. Zimmermann. He thinks she's a screwball, and if she turns up alive, my dad'll never let me go anywhere with Mrs. Zimmermann ever again."

"Oh, now, I think you're being rather hard on your father," said Mrs. Sipes. "I don't know him, of course, but it's hard to believe that he'd think Mrs. Zimmermann was a screwball just because she got lost in the woods. Lots of people get lost, every day."

Yeah, thought Rose Rita, but if he ever found out

Mrs. Zimmermann was a witch, he'd sure go through the roof. Besides he can't help us. Uncle Jonathan is the only one that can. Rose Rita wriggled impatiently and dug her heel into the rug. She felt like a prisoner. If only Mrs. Sipes would just go away so she could call up Uncle Jonathan and find out what to do about Mrs. Bigger! He could give her a magic formula to use, and then everything would be all right. It was all very frustrating. It was like almost having your hands on something and having someone slap your hands away every time you made a grab. She needed that book, the magic book with the funny name. But she couldn't do a thing until Mrs. Sipes left her alone.

While Rose Rita sat there stewing, Mrs. Sipes rattled on about responsibility and honesty, and how your parents were really your best friends if you gave them half a chance. When Rose Rita tuned back in on her, she was saying ". . . And so I think that what we have to do now is call your folks up and tell them what happened. They'll want to know that you're okay. Then I'll drive over to the Gunderson farm and see if everything is all right. You probably left everything wide open, and there are people who just walk in and take things, you know. After that all we can do is wait." Mrs. Sipes walked over and sat down next to Rose Rita on the bed. She put her arm around her. "I'm sorry to have been so hard on you, Rose Rita," she said softly. "I know you must be very upset because of what happened to your friend. But the police are out there now, combing the woods. I'm sure they'll find her."

Fat chance, thought Rose Rita, but again she said nothing. Now if only Mrs. Sipes would get in her car and go over to the farm and leave her here alone! *Go away, Mrs. Sipes! Go away.*

First, though, Rose Rita had to call her folks up. There was no getting around that. The three of them went downstairs, and Rose Rita called up her parents, long distance. Mrs. Pottinger answered the phone, and Rose Rita once again recited her story about how Mrs. Zimmermann had disappeared from the Gunderson farm in the middle of the night and had probably gotten lost in the woods. Mrs. Pottinger was the sort of person who got flustered easily, and when she heard of Mrs. Zimmermann's disappearance, she really got rattled. But she told Rose Rita not to worry, that she and Mr. Pottinger would be up there to get her as soon as they could, and she insisted on being called the moment there was any news about Mrs. Zimmermann. Then Mrs. Sipes took the phone, and she gave Mrs. Pottinger directions for getting to the Sipes farm. After that Mrs. Pottinger talked to Rose Rita a few minutes more, and then she hung up. And then, after a bit of fussing, Mrs. Sipes got into her car and drove off in the direction of the Gunderson farm.

Rose Rita stood by the front window watching Mrs.

Sipes's car as it disappeared over a hill. Aggie stood by her, watching, with her habitual worried expression.

"What're you gonna do now?" she asked.

"I'm gonna call up Lewis's Uncle Jonathan, right away quick. If he doesn't know what to do about old Mrs. Bigger, then nobody does!" Rose Rita felt excited. She already imagined herself armed with a spell and confronting Mrs. Bigger.

Rose Rita went back to the front hall and picked up the telephone. She glanced nervously around to make sure none of the other Sipes kids was in earshot. None of them was. Aggie stood by Rose Rita, anxiously waiting, as she asked for the long distance operator. "I want New Zebedee, Michigan, number 865, please, operator. The residence of Mr. Jonathan Barnavelt. This is a collect call."

Rose Rita and Aggie waited. They could hear the operator ringing Jonathan's phone. *Bzz. Bzz. Bzz.* Eight times she let it ring, and then she said, in that singsongy voice that Rose Rita knew so well, "I am sorry, but the party does not seem to answer. Would you care to call later?"

"Yeah," said Rose Rita, in a dull hopeless voice. "I'll call later. Thanks." She hung up the phone and sat down on the hassock next to the phone table. "Gosh darn!" she said angrily. "Gosh darn it all anyway! *Now* what are we gonna do?"

"Maybe they'll find Mrs. Zimmermann in the forest," said Aggie hopefully. She was having trouble keeping Rose Rita's lies separate from the true story in her head.

Rose Rita just looked at her. "We'll try again," she muttered. "He's got to be home sometime."

Rose Rita tried three more times in ten minutes, but each time the result was the same. After a little while Mrs. Sipes came back. She was beaming, because she had found Mrs. Zimmermann's handbag on the kitchen table in Oley's house, and in the handbag she had found Mrs. Zimmermann's driver's license, her car keys, and a lot of other identification. So now she was convinced that Rose Rita was telling her the whole truth. Rose Rita was glad she was convinced. Now if only Mrs. Sipes would go off to some far corner of her farm, so she could try Jonathan's number again!

But Mrs. Sipes stayed right at home the rest of the day. Rose Rita swung on the front porch swing, and played stickball with Aggie, and helped her feed the cows and slop the hogs. When she wasn't doing anything else, Rose Rita chewed her nails. *Why wouldn't Mrs. Sipes leave?* There was only one phone in the house, and since it was on a table in the front hall, it was hardly private. Mrs. Sipes was not the sort who would stand over Rose Rita while she called, but she might be in the other room, and what would she do if she heard Rose Rita asking Jonathan for a spell that would free Mrs. Zimmermann from Gert Bigger's enchantments? No, she would have to be alone to make a call like that, and Rose Rita knew it. She waited for her chance, but her chance never came.

That evening, as Rose Rita and Aggie helped Mrs. Sipes get dinner ready, the phone rang. It was Mrs. Pottinger. It seemed that their car had broken down on the road. Something had gone wrong with it—the differential, she thought it was. Whatever it was, they wouldn't be in until tomorrow morning. Was there any news about Mrs. Zimmermann? No, there wasn't. Mrs. Pottinger said they were sorry about the delay, but there was no help for it. They'd be there when they got the car running again.

Rose Rita felt like a prisoner who has gotten a stay of execution. Now she would have more time to try to get Uncle Jonathan! "Oh come on, Uncle Jonathan!" she prayed under her breath. "Next time, be home! Please be home! Please!"

Rose Rita spent the evening playing parcheesi and Michigan rummy with Aggie and some of the other Sipes kids. Before she knew it, it was time for bed. She took a bath, which she badly needed, and put on a clean pair of pajamas from her valise, which Mrs. Sipes had brought back from the farmhouse. When Rose Rita was all cleaned up, Mrs. Sipes told her that she was sleeping in the extra bed in Aggie's room. Aggie's room was all flouncy and frilly and pink, a regular girl's room. There was a big teddy bear in the rocking chair in the corner, and there was a vanity table with a round mirror and some perfume bottles on it. Even though she was a farm girl and wore jeans a good deal of the time, Aggie seemed happy to be a girl. She said she looked forward to going to Junior High, and dates and dances and proms and stuff like that. She said that it was a relief sometimes to get out of her jeans and the boots that smelled of manure and go to a square dance at the Four-H Building. Rose Rita wondered if she would think that way herself in the fall. Meanwhile, she had other things on her mind.

That night Rose Rita lay wide awake, listening to the sounds of the house. Her heart was beating fast, and she felt very nervous. The Sipes family went to bed at ten, because they had to be up at six in the morning to do chores. No exceptions were allowed. And considering the fact that there were eight children in the family, the house quieted down pretty fast. By ten-thirty you could have heard a pin drop in the hall.

"Are you awake, Rose Rita?" Aggie hissed.

"Of course I'm awake, you dope. I'm gonna go down in a few minutes and try Uncle Jonathan's number again."

"Do you want me to go with you?"

"No. It'd make too much noise if both of us go. Just sit tight, and wait."

"Okay."

Minutes passed. When Rose Rita was finally sure that the house was asleep, she got out of bed and tiptoed downstairs to the telephone. There was a hall closet near the phone, and fortunately the cord was long. Rose Rita took the phone into the closet, shut the door, and squatted there under the coats. Whispering as loudly as she dared, she asked for Jonathan's number again. Again the operator tried. Ten times, fifteen, twenty times. It was no use. He was away—probably gone for the night.

Rose Rita hung up the phone and put it back on the table. She tiptoed back up the stairs to Aggie's room.

"How'd it go?"

"No soap," Rose Rita whispered. "Maybe he's gone to visit his sister in Osee Five Hills. He does that every now and then, and I don't know her number. I don't even know what her name is. Oh gosh, what are we gonna do?"

"I dunno."

Rose Rita gripped her head with her hands and tried to think. If she could have shaken some thoughts out of her head, she would have done it. There had to be some way, there had to be . . .

"Aggie?"

"Shhh. Not so loud. My ma'll hear us."

Rose Rita tried whispering more softly. "Okay. I'm sorry. Hey, Aggie, listen. Does Mrs. Bigger live in her store? I mean, in back of it, or upstairs?"

"Nope. She lives about two miles down the road in a little house that sets way back from the road. How come you want to know that?"

"Aggie," said Rose Rita in a loud excited whisper, "how'd you like to help me break into Mrs. Bigger's store? Tonight!"

CHAPTER TEN

As soon as Aggie saw what Rose Rita's plan was, she tried to back out. She thought up a thousand reasons for not going to Mrs. Bigger's place, that night or any other night. They might get caught and put in reform school. Aggie's mom would catch them, and bawl them out, and tell Rose Rita's folks. Mrs. Bigger might be there, hiding in a closet and waiting for them. The store would be all locked up, and they wouldn't be able to get in. They might get bitten by Mrs. Bigger's dog. And so on and so forth. But Rose Rita was not impressed by Aggie's arguments. She had only known Aggie for a short while, but she knew by now that Aggie was a worrywart. Worrywarts always imagine that terrible things are going to happen. They imagine dangers where dangers don't exist. Lewis was a worrywart, and he was always fussing and fretting about something. Right now Aggie was acting just like Lewis.

To Rose Rita everything seemed clear. Mrs. Bigger was a witch, and she was always reading magic books. She probably had a copy of the Mallet of Whatever-it-was, the book that Rose Rita had to have if she was going to save Mrs. Zimmermann. It might be in her home, or it might be in her store somewhere. It was very likely to be in her store, since she spent a lot of time there and probably read while she worked. After all, Rose Rita argued, she had found that magic charm tucked away in one of Gert Bigger's account books. Well, if she had found that, she might find other things. Rose Rita ignored the holes in her argument. She didn't want to see them. Already she was beginning to be carried away by the idea of bearding Gert Bigger in her den. She imagined herself armed with a great book from which she read strange grim-sounding incantations, magic words that would bring Gert Bigger to her knees and make her bring Mrs. Zimmermann back from . . . from wherever Gert Bigger had sent her. It occurred to Rose Rita, of course, that maybe Mrs. Bigger had used her magic to kill Mrs. Zimmermann. Well, thought Rose Rita grimly, if she's done that, I'll make her bring Mrs. Zimmermann back—back from the dead. And if I can't do that, I'll make her pay for what she did. A tremendous anger was building in Rose Rita's mind. Righteous anger. She hated that big rawboned woman with the nasty sneering manner and the insults and lies and dirty rotten cheating ways. She was going to fix her, and fix her good. In the meantime, however, she had to persuade Aggie to go along with her plan. It wasn't easy. Rose Rita argued and wheedled, but Aggie was a stubborn girl—about as stubborn as Rose Rita. And Aggie was especially stubborn when she was scared.

"All right, Aggie," said Rose Rita, folding her arms and glaring. "If *that's* the way you're gonna be, I'll just go by myself!"

Aggie looked hurt. "You mean it? Really?"

Rose Rita nodded grimly. "Uh-huh. Try and stop me."

Actually, Aggie could have stopped Rose Rita easily, and Rose Rita knew it. All she had to do was shout, and Mrs. Sipes, who was a very light sleeper, would be down in the room asking them what all the racket was about. But Aggie didn't shout. She really did want to be in on the adventure. On the other hand, she was afraid.

"Come on, Aggie," Rose Rita pleaded. "We won't get caught, I promise you. And if we get our hands on a copy of that book I told you about, we can really fix old Mrs. Bigger's wagon. You'd like that, wouldn't you?"

Aggie's forehead wrinkled up. Her eyebrows got so worried that they almost met. "Gee, I still don't know, Rose Rita. Are you sure that whatchamacallit book'll be there?"

"Of course I'm not sure, dopey. But we'll never find out if we sit here all night. Come on, Aggie. Please!"

Aggie looked uncertain. "Well, how're we gonna get in? The doors and windows'll all be locked."

"We can figure that out when we get there. Maybe we'll have to break a window or something."

"It'd make a lot of noise," said Aggie. "And you might cut yourself on the glass."

"We'll pick the lock then. People do it all the time in the movies."

"This isn't the movies, this is real life. Do you know how to pick locks? Huh? Do you? I bet you don't."

Rose Rita felt totally exasperated. "Look, Aggie," she said, "if we get there and we can't find any way to get in, we can give up and come back. Okay? And if there is a way to get in, you won't even have to come inside with me. You can stay outside and be the lookout. Come on, Aggie. I really need you. How about it? Huh?"

Aggie scratched her head and looked uncertain. "You promise I won't have to come in with you? And if we can't get in, we'll come straight back here?"

Rose Rita drew a cross on her stomach with her finger. "I promise. Cross my heart and hope to die."

"Okay," said Aggie. "Wait'll I get my flashlight. We'll need it."

Working as quietly as they could, Rose Rita and Aggie got into their clothes and put on their sneakers. Aggie dug a long-barreled flashlight out of her closet and poked around in her dresser drawer till she found an old boy scout knife. It had a black wrinkly plastic handle, and inside a little glass bubble at one end of the handle was a compass. Aggie really couldn't say why she was taking along this particular piece of equipment, but she thought it might come in handy.

When they were all ready, the two girls tiptoed to the door of the bedroom. Aggie led the way. Carefully she opened the door, just a crack, and looked out.

"Okay!" she whispered. "Just follow me."

The two girls tiptoed down the hall and down the stairs. They walked softly through rooms that lay gleaming in moonlight till they reached the back door. The back door was propped open because it was a hot night, and the screen door was unhooked. They went out, closing the door softly behind them.

"Wow!" breathed Rose Rita. "That part was easy!"

Aggie smiled shyly. "Yeah. I've done it before. I used to go frog-spearin' with my brother down to the crick there, but my mom caught us and gave us heck. I haven't been out in the middle of the night since then. Come on."

Aggie and Rose Rita started walking down a rutty wagon road that ran between two plowed fields. They climbed a little fence and trotted along a grassy track that ran parallel to the main road. Rose Rita saw at once that they were going back by the way they had come on the previous day when Aggie found Rose Rita sleeping next to the cornfield. Now the field was on their left, rustling softly in the night breeze. Stars were clustered thick overhead, and crickets chirped in the tall grass.

Before long the girls passed the place where they had met. There was the droopy elm tree and the flat-topped boulder. They had been chattering excitedly, but now they grew quiet. They were not far from Mrs. Bigger's store.

At the edge of the gravel road the two girls paused. There was Gert Bigger's grocery store, shut up for the night. A yellow insect lamp lit up the front door, and through the wide plate glass window the girls could see a night light burning in the rear of the store. The sign with the flying red horse creaked gently in the wind, and the two gas pumps looked like soldiers on guard.

"Here we are," whispered Aggie.

"Yeah," said Rose Rita. She felt something tighten up in her stomach. Maybe this was a dumb plan after all. She was about to ask Aggie if she really felt like going ahead with their plan, but she swallowed her fears and crossed the road. Aggie followed, glancing about her nervously.

"It looks okay," said Aggie, when they were both on the other side of the road. "Her car's always parked over there when she's here, and it's gone."

"Good! Do you think we ought to try the front door?"

"Well, you can if you want to. But I'm sure it'll be locked."

Rose Rita trotted up the steps and rattled the door. It was locked. Locked tight. She shrugged and ran back down the steps.

"Come on, Aggie. That's one down, and a lot to go. It's such a hot night that she might have left one window open. Let's check the windows." Rose Rita could feel her courage and her habitual optimism coming back. Everything would work out all right. They'd find a way in.

Apparently Rose Rita's optimism was catching. Aggie brightened up and became—for her—confident. "Hey, that's an idea! Okay, we'll check."

As they passed around the side of the building, the girls heard a loud clucking sound. There behind the fence was that poor bedraggled white chicken. It looked even more beat-up and scrawny than it had when Rose Rita saw it the day before. Old Gertie oughta feed it, Rose Rita thought. As before, the hen was very excited. It ran back and forth behind the fence, clucking and flapping its wings.

"Oh be quiet!" Rose Rita hissed. "We're not gonna chop off your head! Just cool down, for heaven's sake!"

The two girls started to inspect the windows on the side of the house. The ones on the first floor were shut tight, and it was likely they were locked as well. Just to make sure Rose Rita got up on an orange crate and tried to move one of them. It wouldn't budge an inch.

"Darn it all anyway!" she grumbled as she got down off the crate.

"Oh, don't give up yet!" said Aggie. "We haven't tried the . . . oops. Watch out!"

Rose Rita whirled around in time to see a car pass by. Its headlights swept across the side of the store and were gone. If the driver had been paying attention, he would have seen the two figures standing next to the store. But, apparently, he had not noticed. Rose Rita felt exposed, as if she were in a fishbowl. She felt the danger of what she was doing.

"C'mon," she said, tugging nervously at Aggie's arm. "Let's go around to the back."

The two girls walked around to the rear of the store. The little white hen, which had never stopped squawking since the time they arrived, kept it up until they disappeared around the corner of the building. Rose Rita was glad when it finally shut up. It was beginning to make her nervous.

The two girls tried the back door. It was locked. Then they stepped back and surveyed the rear wall of the building. The first floor windows had heavy iron grills over them—probably they were the windows of the storeroom, where the groceries were kept. There was one window on the second floor, and—Rose Rita stepped back to make sure—yes, it was open! Not wide open, but open a crack.

"Wow!" said Rose Rita, pointing. "Do you see that?"

Aggie looked doubtful. "Yeah, I do, but I don't see how you could wiggle in through a crack like that."

"I'm not gonna wiggle in through the crack, dumbo! That crack means that the window isn't fastened. So if I climb up there, I can open it up."

"How you gonna do that?"

Rose Rita looked around. "I dunno yet. Let's see if there's anything to climb up on."

Rose Rita and Aggie poked around in the back yard of Gert Bigger's store for a while, but they didn't find any ladders. There was a toolshed, but it had a padlock on it. Rose Rita went back to the window and peered up at it owlishly. She rubbed her chin.

There was an apple tree growing near the store, and one of its branches nearly touched the sill of the window she wanted. But Rose Rita was an experienced tree climber, and she knew that the branch would start to bend as soon as she tried to climb out on it. By the time she got near the end of the branch, it would be bent way down. So that was no good. On the other hand there was a trellis nailed to the side of the house. It ran right up next to the window. If she could climb up on it, she might be able to get hold of the sill and swing herself over. It was worth a try.

Rose Rita took a deep breath and flexed her hands. She walked up to the trellis. It was covered with thick thorny vines, but there were places, here and there, where you could put your hands. Rose Rita put a foot on one slat and a hand on another. She swung herself up so her weight was on the trellis, and hung there, waiting to see what would happen. Nails skreeked as the trellis started to pull out from the wall.

"It doesn't look too good," said Aggie, screwing up her mouth into a very worried scowl. "If you climb any farther, you're gonna break your neck."

Rose Rita said nothing. The trellis was still attached to the wall, so she put another foot up. Then another foot, and another hand. With a loud splintering, crackling, rustling, and squeaking noise, the trellis leaned lazily sideways. Nails and broken pieces of wood dropped to the ground. Rose Rita leaped free of the wreckage and landed on her feet. Aggie, with a little cry, dropped the knife in the grass and ran to Rose Rita's side. She found her standing there, sucking a cut thumb and glaring hatefully at the ruined trellis.

"Darned thorns anyway!" Rose Rita grumbled.

"Gee, is she ever gonna be ticked off!" said Aggie. "Mrs. Bigger, I mean."

Rose Rita wasn't listening. She was wondering if maybe she could scale the side of the building. It wasn't very far up to the second story, and the white clapboard strips looked as though they might give her a handhold. She tried, but she slid down. She tried again, with the same result. She stood there, panting and redfaced. For the first time, she doubted the wisdom of her plan.

"Let's go home," said Rose Rita bitterly. She felt the tears stinging her eyes.

"Are you giving up already?" said Aggie. "Gee, I don't think that's a very good idea. We haven't looked at the other side of the store."

Rose Rita gave a start and looked at Aggie. She was right! Rose Rita had been so wrapped up in the problem of the upstairs window that she had forgotten all about the far side of the building, the one side that they hadn't checked out yet. Hope and optimism came flowing back.

"Okay. Let's go look," said Rose Rita, grinning.

On the far side of the store thick bushes grew up close to the windows, but there was a little tunnel in the shrubbery where you could sidle in if you hunkered down a bit. Rose Rita and Aggie bent over and edged their way in under the bushes. They looked up and saw that the windows on this side had grates and padlocks like the ones on the back of the store. But down at ground level was a cellar entrance. The old-fashioned kind, with two slanting wooden doors. Aggie shone her flashlight over the door. There was a pair of metal fixtures where the two doors met. Obviously they were meant to hold a padlock, but there was no padlock in the holes. The door was unlocked.

Cautiously Rose Rita gripped the handle of one of the heavy wooden doors. She lifted it, and a smell of earth and mold rose to her nostrils. It was like a breath from the grave. Rose Rita shuddered and stepped back. She

dropped the door. It fell with a loud clatter.

Aggie gave Rose Rita a frightened look. "What's wrong, Rose Rita? Did you see something?"

Rose Rita passed a hand over her forehead. She felt dizzy. "I . . . no, I didn't, Aggie, only . . . only I got scared. I d'no why, but I did. I guess I'm just a scaredy-cat, that's all."

"It's funny, isn't it?" Aggie mused, as she stared down at the door. "All those bars and locks on everything else, and she leaves this open. It's weird."

"Yeah. Maybe she didn't think anyone'd go pokin' around under these bushes." Rose Rita realized that this was a pretty weak explanation, but it was the only one she could come up with. There was something very strange about this open door. She just couldn't figure it out.

Suddenly Rose Rita thought of something. She picked up the cellar door again and opened it all the way. She opened the other door panel too. Then she took the flashlight from Aggie and stepped down into the dark opening. At the bottom of a short flight of stone steps Rose Rita found a black door with a dirty cobwebbed window. She put her hand on the porcelain knob and found that it felt surprisingly cold. Rose Rita turned the knob and pushed cautiously. At first she thought the door was locked, but when she pushed harder, it opened with a loud dismal rattle.

Inside the cellar it was pitch-dark. Rose Rita played the beam of her flashlight around and saw vague shapes hunched in the gloom.

"Are you okay?" called Aggie nervously.

"Yeah, I . . . I think so. Look, Aggie. You stay up here and keep watch. I'm goin' in and have a look around."

"Don't stay too long."

"Don't worry, I won't. See you later."

"Okay."

Rose Rita turned and flashed her light up. There stood Aggie with her worried frown. She was waving feebly. Rose Rita swallowed hard and thought about Mrs. Zimmermann. She turned and went in.

As she crossed the cold stone floor, Rose Rita glanced nervously from side to side. In one corner a furnace squatted. With its upraised metal arms, it looked like some kind of monster. Near it was a freezer. It reminded Rose Rita of a tomb. She laughed nervously. Why did everything seem so scary? This was a perfectly ordinary basement. There weren't any ghosts or monsters in it. Rose Rita walked on.

In a far corner of the basement she found a flight of wooden steps leading up. Slowly she climbed. The steps creaked loudly under her feet. At the top of the steps was a door. Rose Rita opened it and looked out. She was in the store.

Groceries stood piled in shadowy ranks. Cans, bottles,

jars, and boxes, half lit by the weak little bulb that burned over the cash register. Outside the wide front window a car passed. Rose Rita could hear a clock ticking slowly, but she couldn't see it. She walked across the room and opened a door. Here were steps leading up. She started to climb.

Halfway up the steps Rose Rita noticed something that made her stop: a picture hanging with its face turned to the wall. Curious, she reached up and turned it over. The picture showed a saint with a halo. He was clutching a cross and staring up toward heaven with wide unearthly eyes. Hurriedly Rose Rita turned the picture back toward the wall. A violent shudder passed through her body. Why had she been so frightened? She didn't know. When she had calmed down, she went on up the stairs.

At the top of the steps was an L-shaped hallway, and halfway along it was a paneled door. There was a key sticking out of the door. She turned it, and the door swung open. Rose Rita waved her flashlight around, and found that she was in a small bedroom.

There was a light switch just inside the door. Rose Rita's hand moved toward it, but then she stopped. Would it be a bad thing to turn the light on? She glanced toward the window. It was the only one in the room, the window she had tried to reach by climbing the trellis. The window looked out on the dark mass of trees behind the store. Gert Bigger was miles away. If I turn on the light, Rose Rita thought, people will just figure it's old Gertie up here counting her money. She snapped the switch and started looking around.

It was a very ordinary room. The only thing odd about it was its lived-in look, but it occurred to Rose Rita that maybe Gert Bigger stayed here during the winter, on nights when the weather was so bad that it was impossible to drive home. In one corner stood a small iron bed. It was painted green, and the wrought iron posies on the bars of the headboard were touched up in pink. Nearby was a closet without any door. Ordinary ladies' dresses hung on the rack, and wadded nylons lay on the floor near a heavy-looking pair of black ladies' shoes. There was a shelf in the closet, and something like a blanket lay folded up on it. Nothing unusual here.

Rose Rita walked across the room and examined the dresser. There was a mirror on top of it, and in front of the mirror was a collection of bottles and jars. Jergen's lotion, Noxzema, Pond's lotion, and a big blue bottle of Evening in Paris perfume. On the white linen runner lay tweezers and combs and brushes, and bits of tissue paper, and little curls of dark brown hair. There was a box of Kleenex, too.

Rose Rita turned and gazed around the room. Was there anything else here? There was. On a low table next to the bed was a large book. A big heavy book with a tooled leather cover. The pages were edged with gilt, and there were fussy gilded decorations on the spine and on the cover. A soiled red marker was sticking out of the book.

Rose Rita could hear her heart beating. She swallowed hard. Could this be it? She went closer, and opened the heavy front cover. Her face fell. It wasn't the book she wanted. It was something called *A Cyclopaedia of Jewish Antiquities*, by the Reverend Merriwether Burchard, D.D., Litt.D. Well, at least it was a book of some sort. Rose Rita started leafing through it.

The book was printed in double columns of tiny black print, and it was full of dark mysterious engravings. According to the captions, the pictures showed The Temple of Solomon, the Ark of the Covenant, the Brazen Laver, the Seven-Branched Candlestick, and things like that. Rose Rita knew what some of the things in the pictures were. There were engravings like these in her grandmother's family Bible. Rose Rita yawned. It looked like a pretty boring book. She looked around and sighed. This certainly wasn't any witch's den. Maybe she was wrong about Gert Bigger being a witch. Rose Rita realized, with a sinking heart, that her witch theory was based on a lot of guesswork. Mrs. Bigger might have had a picture of Mordecai Hunks on her wall, but what did that prove? As for the photo Mrs. Zimmermann had found, it might all have been just a coincidence. As for the strange drawing and Mrs. Bigger's odd reading habits, well, she might just be one of those people who want to be a witch. Mrs. Zimmermann had told Rose Rita once that there were lots of people who would love to have magical powers, although there wasn't chance in a million that they would ever get them. People like that would read magic books in hopes of getting to be magicians, wouldn't they? Well, wouldn't they?

Rose Rita began to wonder if she hadn't made a terrible mistake. Some strange things had happened to her and Mrs. Zimmermann, but that didn't mean that old Mrs. Bigger had made them happen. She picked up her flashlight off the bed and was about to go downstairs when she heard a noise. A faint scratching at the door of the bedroom.

Terror gripped Rose Rita for an instant, and then she remembered something that made her laugh. Mrs. Bigger had a dog. A small black dog. Probably she had locked it in the store for the night.

With a sigh of relief, Rose Rita opened the door. It was the dog, all right. It trotted across the room and hopped up on the bed. Rose Rita smiled and turned toward the door. But she stopped again, because the dog had made a very odd sound. A sound very much like a human being coughing. Animals sometimes make human sounds. The cries of cats are, on certain occasions, just like a baby's wails. Rose Rita knew that, but still the sound made her stop. The hair on the back of her neck stood up on end. She turned slowly around. There on the bed sat Gert Bigger. Her hard brutal mouth was set in the evilest of smiles.

CHAPTER ELEVEN

Rose Rita lay in darkness. She felt a slight pressure on her eyes and knew that there was something covering them, but she didn't know what it was. She would have reached up to uncover her eyes, but she couldn't. Her hands were crossed on her breast, and though she could feel them, she couldn't move them. She couldn't move any part of her body, nor could she speak, but she could hear, and she could feel. As she lay there, a fly—it felt like a fly—landed on her forehead and walked the length of her nose before buzzing away.

Where was she? Probably in the bedroom above Gert Bigger's store. It felt as if she was lying on a bed, anyway. And there was a blanket, or something like a blanket, drawn up over her body. It felt heavy, and the room was hot and still. Tiny rivulets of sweat ran down Rose Rita's body. Why couldn't she move? Was she paralyzed, or what? There came back to her now, like a bad dream, the terror she had felt when she saw Gert Bigger sitting on the bed, leering at her. She must have fainted then, because she could not remember anything after that.

Rose Rita heard a lock click. A door creaked open. Heavy footfalls crossed the room and stopped next to her head. A chair creaked.

"Well, well, well. And how are you, Miss Nosy? Hmmm? Not speaking to me? That's not nice. You know, I'm the one who ought to be insulted, the way you broke in here and rummaged around. Were you tryin' to find out if I was a witch? Well, you can relax. I am."

Gert Bigger laughed, and it was not at all the kind of laugh that you would expect to come out of a big husky woman like her. It was a high-pitched tinny giggle. Rose Rita thought it sounded like the laughter of a crazy person.

"Yes, sirree," Gert Bigger went on, "it all started when that old fool of a Gunderson dropped in here one night. He was half-crocked, and he started talkin' about this magic ring he had found on his farm. Well, at first I thought he was just foolin', but I got to thinkin' later—what if it's the truth? You see, I've always wanted to be able to work magic. I've studied up on it a lot. Well, after old Oley kicked off, I broke into his place and hunted around till I found the darned thing. It's on my finger right now. Did you read in that book what that fella Burchard said about it? It's all true, you know, every word. Here, let me read it to you."

Rose Rita heard the sound of fingers riffling through the pages of a book. "Here it is, where I stuck the marker. You must've seen it when you were pokin' around, though sometimes you nosy types don't see what's right under your nose." She giggled again. "Ready? Here it is. '. . . No account of Jewish antiquities would be complete without mention of the legendary ring of King Solomon. According to the great historian Flavius Josephus, King Solomon possessed a magic ring that enabled him to do many wonderful things. The ring gave him the power of teleportation, that is, the ability to be whisked from place to place, unseen. It conferred upon him the powers of sorcery and divination, and enabled him to humiliate his enemies by changing them into lowly beasts. In this manner, it is said, King Solomon brought low the king of the Hittites, when he turned him into an ox. The ring also enabled Solomon to change his own shape at will—his most favored form is said to have been that of a small black dog, in which shape he prowled about, spying on his enemies and finding out many secrets. But the greatest power of the ring was one which Solomon, wisest of men, never chose to use. The ring could, if the wearer desired it, give long life and great beauty. To obtain this gift, however, the wearer was obliged to call upon the demon Asmodai. It may be for this reason that Solomon refused to exercise this power of the ring. For, we are told, he who sups with the Devil . . .' "

The book slammed shut. "That's enough of you, Reverend," muttered Gert Bigger. "Well, there you are, Miss Nosy. Isn't that interestin'? But I'll tell you what is most interestin' of all. You came here at just the right time, you really did. I was goin' to do somethin' to you when I caught you pokin' around in my back room, but later, I says to myself, I says, 'She'll be back!' And you did come back, you did, you did!" Gert Bigger let out a peal of shrill laughter. "I left the padlock off of my cellar door, and you went right in, like the little fool that you are. Well, you're gonna find out what it's like to monkey around with witches. Florence found out, and I'm not through with her yet, not by a long shot." She paused and made an unpleasant spitting sound. "Phah! Oh, didn't I know, didn't I know what she was up to when she showed up here, pretendin' she was out of gas! I knew about her and all that magic monkey-do of hers, that college degree and all, and I says to myself, 'She's after the ring!' I was real worried then, because I didn't know how to handle the ring proper, cept'n for the black-dog trick. Well, after you folks went up north, I learned. I sent that photograft up there, and that was me you saw in Florence's room. I showed up in the back seat o' your car for a coupla seconds too. Scared the dickens out o'you, didn't I?" She laughed shrilly. Then, after another pause, she continued, in a grimmer tone, "Well, fun's fun, but I'm through playin' around. I've got Florence, and I'm gonna fix her good, so she'll never be able to get my ring from me, not ever!

"A course," she added, "I've got a special grudge against her for makin' my life miserable. If me'n Mordy had got married, my life would've been better. The old fool that I was married to used to beat me up. You don't know what it was like. You don't know at all." Gert Bigger's voice cracked. Was she crying? Rose Rita couldn't tell.

Gert Bigger rambled on, in her hard angry voice. She explained to Rose Rita that she had put her under a death spell. When dawn came, she would die. They would find her body here surrounded by the paraphernalia of Gert Bigger's magic. But Gert Bigger would be gone. In fact there would be no Gert Bigger, because she would be a young beautiful woman. She had it all figured out: she would go away to another place and change her name. She had drawn all her money out of the bank— it was in the safe downstairs. With a new name and a new life she could start making up for all the rotten things that had happened to her. And before she left, she would settle accounts with Florence Zimmermann, for good and for all.

After she had finished talking, Gert Bigger left the room and locked the door. Rose Rita stared hopelessly into the darkness that lay around her. She thought about Aggie. Aggie was her only hope. Rose Rita had no idea how much time had gone by since she left Aggie standing outside the cellar door. She hoped that Gert Bigger hadn't captured Aggie too. Rose Rita prayed, though her mouth stayed shut and no sound came out. Please, God, help Aggie to find me. Make her get help before it's too late. Please God please . . .

A long time passed. At least it seemed like a long time, though Rose Rita had no way of telling how long it was. Her wristwatch was still on her wrist, ticking, but it did her no good. How would she know when it was dawn? She would know when she was dead. Tick-tick-tick-tick. Rose Rita could feel her body growing numb. She couldn't feel her hands on her breast any more. She had a horrible vision of herself as a severed head lying on a pillow. It was such an awful thought that she tried to get rid of it, but it kept coming back. Please, God, send Aggie, send somebody. Tick-tick-tick-tick . . .

Brr-rrr-rrring. A doorbell was ringing. It rang several times, and then Rose Rita heard the muffled tinkling of the little bell above the door of the store. She heard nothing after that—if people were talking, she couldn't hear them. Silence. More time passed. Then Rose Rita heard the lock on the bedroom door click. Footsteps, and the creak of a chair as somebody heavy sat down.

"My lord, it takes all kinds to make a world!" said Gert Bigger. "Who do you suppose I've just been talkin' to? Guess. Give up? Mrs. Sipes, who lives down the road. Her and her daughter . . . Aggie I think is her name. They were all wrought up because Aggie said I kidnaped you. Imagine that!" Gert Bigger giggled. "They had even brought a cop along with 'em to search the place. Well, I know my rights. He didn't have no search warrant, and I told him so. I says to him, I know my rights and you can't come in, and no, I don't know nothin' about no little girl! So there! Imagine the nerve of 'em, comin' here like that!" Gert Bigger laughed again. The chair creaked as she rocked back and forth, laughing. The tiny flame of hope in Rose Rita's mind flickered out. She was going to die, and there was nothing that anyone could do about it.

Gert Bigger left the room, and there was another long dark silence. Rose Rita kept hearing little sounds, but she couldn't figure out what they were. Finally the door creaked open again, and she heard Gert Bigger walking around the room. She was humming to herself, and there was a sound of drawers opening and shutting. She was packing up, getting ready to leave. After what seemed like a long time, Rose Rita heard the latches of a suitcase snap shut. Gert Bigger walked over to her chair by the head of the bed and sat down again.

"How're you doin'? Hmm? Feel anything yet? This spell comes over you gradual-like, or so I'm told. But it

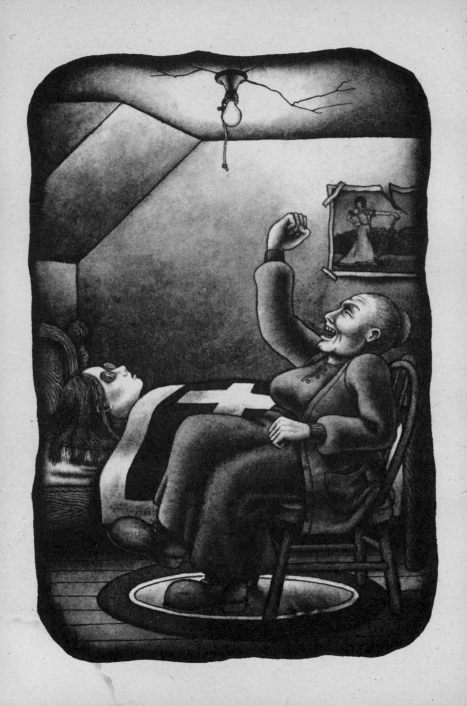

won't be over with till dawn, and that's still a ways off yet. Okay now. I'm all ready to go. I haven't taken care of Florence yet, but I think I'll do that on my way out. I want her to see what I'm like after I've been changed. And you know what? Seeing as how you've been so nice and quiet, I'm gonna let you watch me do my little quick-change act. Well, uh, of course I'm kiddin' in a way, because I really can't let you see me. I'd have to take those things off of your eyes, and that would break the spell, and we can't have that, can we? No sir-ree. But I tell you what I'll do. I'll sit right here in this chair and summon up old Asmodai, and you can hear his voice. How'll that be? Let me see now, what is it that I do? Oh yes . . ."

Gert Bigger clapped her hands three times and said in a loud commanding voice, "Send Asmodai to me! Now!"

At first nothing happened. Then, slowly, Rose Rita began to feel the presence of something evil. Feeling returned to her body. Her flesh was covered with goose bumps, and she felt cold. The air grew thick, and it was hard to breathe. Out of the darkness a harsh whispery voice spoke.

"Who calls upon Asmodai?"

"I do. I am wearing the ring of King Solomon, and I want to be changed. I want to be young and beautiful, and I want to live for a thousand years." Gert added quickly, "But I don't want to get old. I want to stay young, all the time."

"So be it," said the whispery voice.

As soon as the whispery voice had finished speaking, Rose Rita heard a small sound. It was a sound like somebody dropping a quarter on the floor. Then there was a sound like a strong wind roaring through the room. The room trembled, as if the ground underneath the building was quaking. Rose Rita heard all sorts of rattling clattering sounds. The bed shook, and whatever had been on her eyes slid off. She sat up and shook her head groggily. Rose Rita looked around. Where were her glasses? What had Gert Bigger done with them? She groped around on the nightstand and found them. She put them on and glanced around. Gert Bigger was gone. She had not heard her go out, and the key was sticking out of the inside of the door. On the bed next to her, Rose Rita saw two silver dollars. They must have been the things over her eyes. And she found that she was lying under a heavy black woolen blanket. It had a white border and a big white cross on it. Rose Rita knew what it was. She had been to a funeral at the Catholic church in New Zebedee, and she had seen a casket covered with a blanket just like this one. With a violent shudder she thrust the thing away from her and sat up.

Rose Rita felt sick. She felt like somebody who has been in bed with the flu for two weeks. When she tried to stand up, she sat down again suddenly. Sweat was pouring down her face. As she gazed woozily around the room, it occurred to her to wonder just what had happened to Mrs. Bigger. Probably she had had her wish granted, and she was out in Hollywood, living it up with Lana Turner and Esther Williams and all that crowd. Rose Rita didn't know, and she didn't care. She felt dizzy, and she couldn't stop shuddering. Her head was as light as a wicker basket. Finally, with an effort, she forced herself to stand up. Now she remembered something, something that had puzzled her. That sound, like a coin hitting the floor. What was it? Rose Rita got down on her hands and knees and looked under the bed. And at that moment she heard, from downstars, a terrific pounding and banging. The doorbell rang about eight times, and a muffled voice yelled, "Open up! Open up in the name of the law!" They were back! Aggie and her mom and the cops! Rose Rita glanced toward the door. What if Mrs. Bigger had left her ring behind? Wouldn't it be great to be able to run downstairs to meet Aggie with the ring of King Solomon in her fist? Rose Rita bent over and scrabbled in the dust under the bed. There it was! She reached out and hooked the ring with her finger. Now she drew the ring to her and closed her fist around it.

And with that something happened. A shudder ran through Rose Rita's body, and she felt . . . well, *strange*. She felt proud and bitter and angry, angry at the people who had come to drag her back to her old life.

"Okay, Mrs. Bigger," the voice boomed. "We're gonna give you a count of ten before we break the door down! One . . ."

Rose Rita got up and glared fiercely at the door. The expression on her face was so hateful that she hardly looked like herself at all. A wild light was in her eyes. So they were coming to get her! Well, they'd have to catch her first. She rushed to the door and unlocked it. With the ring still clutched tight in her fist, Rose Rita dashed out into the hall. At the far end of the hall was a half-opened door, and she could see stairs leading down. It wasn't the staircase she had come up by, it was another one, leading to the back of the building. Rose Rita ran toward it.

"Six . . . seven . . ."

Down the stairs she clattered. At the bottom was a door with a night lock and a chain. Working furiously, yet never letting the ring out of her hand for a second, Rose Rita undid the locks and chains and bolts.

"Ten!" There was a loud crash and a babble of voices shouting. In the middle of it all Rose Rita heard Aggie yelling "Rose Rita! Are you all right?" Rose Rita hesitated. She glanced waveringly toward the front of the store, where all the noise was coming from. Then her face hardened, and she gripped the ring tighter. Rose Rita turned and ran, out past the toolshed and the clothesline, toward the dark mass of trees that grew right up to the edge of Gert Bigger's back yard. The shadow of the pines seemed to reach out and swallow her up.

CHAPTER TWELVE

Rose Rita ran through the woods, her feet slapping the ground under her. Bits and pieces of scenery jolted past, branches and stumps, and fungi laddering tall dark trunks. She ran on a crooked path covered with brown pine needles, a path that wound deeper and deeper into the woods. Sometimes she fell or barked her shins on a stump, but each time she got up and kept on running. Faster and faster she ran. Branches whipped across her face and arms, leaving angry red marks, but the pain of the cuts just made her run faster. As she ran, her mind was filled with a wild jumble of thoughts. Images leaped before her, like flashes of lightning. Rose Rita saw them as clearly as if they had been printed on the air. She saw the boy with the crew cut who had yelled, "You're a pretty funny kind of a girl!" She saw the girls standing on the sidelines at the Saturday night dance. She saw the black prison-like junior high building where she had to go next fall. She saw girls in flouncy dresses, girls who wore nylons and lipstick and mascara, asking her, "What's the matter with you? Don't you want to go on dates? Dating is fun!"

As Rose Rita ran, she thought she could hear someone behind her, calling her name. The voice was faint and far-off, but she was sure she had heard it call to her once or twice. No, Rose Rita panted. You're not gonna get me. I've had about enough, I've had about enough, and I'm gonna get what I want . . .

On and on Rose Rita ran, pell-mell, through the dark pine forest. She left the path behind and half slid, half ran down a steep bank. The bank was covered with pine needles, and pine needles are slippery. She lost her footing and tumbled, head over heels. Over and over she rolled. When she got to the bottom, dazed and sick and shaken, the first thing she did was make sure that she had the ring with her. There it was, still clutched tight in her fist. Rose Rita opened her hand only long enough to make sure the ring was safe. Then she closed her fist tight, staggered to her feet, and started running again. There was something inside her head that kept driving her on, something relentless and mechanical, like a piston.

Go on, go on, it said. Keep going, keep going, keep going, keep going . . .

Rose Rita splashed across a shallow little stream and started to climb the bank on the other side. But the bank was steep, and it was hard climbing with one hand doubled up into a fist. Rose Rita paused, panting, half-way up. Why not put the ring on? She opened her hand and gaped stupidly at the small heavy object. It was too big—it would fall off her finger. How about putting it in her pocket? No, there might be a hole in the pocket. It might get lost. She had to know, all the time, that it was there. Rose Rita closed up her fist and climbed on, one-handed. She was a good climber, and there were roots here and there that could be used like the rungs of a ladder. Up she went. When she got to the top she paused to catch her breath.

"Rose Rita! Rose Rita! Stop!"

Rose Rita whirled. Who was that? It was a voice she knew. She was on the point of turning back when that driving piston in her head started up again. Go on, go on, go on, let's go, let's go, let's go. Rose Rita glared back across the stream. There was wild insane anger in her eyes now. "Come and get me!" she snarled through her teeth. Then she turned and ran on.

On into the forest Rose Rita plunged. But now her legs were starting to give out. They felt like rubber. Lying under that spell on Gert Bigger's bed had weakened her, the way a long illness would have. Her side hurt, and when she tried to catch her breath, watery bubbles kept bursting in her mouth. She was wringing wet with sweat, and her glasses were fogged up. Rose Rita wanted to stop, but the driving piston wouldn't let her. It forced her on until, finally, she reeled out into a little clearing. Rose Rita fell to her knees and looked around. Where was she? What was she doing? Oh, yes, she was going to . . . she was going . . . to . . . The world was starting to spin around her. Dark trees and starlit sky and gray grass whizzed past, like the things you see out of a car window when you're going very fast. Rose Rita fell down on her back and passed out.

The first thing that Rose Rita saw when she woke up, some time later, was a small cold pale moon shining down on her. She sat up and shook her head. All around her the dark trees stood, a ring of shadows cutting off escape. But she didn't want to escape, did she? No. She had come here to do something, but she couldn't for the life of her remember what it was. Rose Rita felt a pain in her left hand. She picked her fist up off the grass and stared at it as if it was something that belonged to somebody else. Slowly she opened her stiff cramped painful fingers. In her palm lay a large battered ring. She had been holding it so long, and so tight, that it had dug a deep red welt into her hand.

Wincing, Rose Rita turned the ring over with her fingers. It was made of gold—at least it seemed to be. And it was a signet ring. There was a design cut into the flat surface on the top. A face. A staring face with blank eyeballs and lips curled into a cold evil smile. Rose Rita was fascinated by the face. It seemed so lifelike. She half expected to see the lips part and to hear a voice speak.

And then she remembered why she was here.

Rose Rita stood up, swaying, in the gray moonlit clearing. She slid the ring onto the third finger of her left hand and held it there so it wouldn't fall off. Rose Rita gasped. The ring had shrunk to fit her hand! But she had no time to think of these things. A voice was in her head, telling her what to do. She clapped three times in weak imitation of Mrs. Bigger and said, in as loud a voice as she could manage, "I . . . I call upon As . . . Asmodai! Come to me! Now!"

A shadow fell across the gray starlit grass. And Rose Rita heard the harsh whispery voice that she had heard in Gert Bigger's room.

"I am called Asmodai. What do you want?"

Rose Rita shivered. She felt cold and frightened and alone. She wanted to rip the ring from her hand and throw it away. But she couldn't. An insistent angry voice, her own voice inside her head, went on talking. It told her what she had to do. It told her that she had to change, that she could solve all her problems now if only she had the courage. It also told her that she would only have this one chance, and that she'd never get another.

The whispery voice spoke again. It sounded faintly impatient. "I am called Asmodai. What do you want? You are the wielder of the ring of Solomon. What do you want?"

"I . . . I want . . . what I want to do is . . . what I want is . . ."

"Rose Rita, stop! Stop what you're doing and look at me!"

Rose Rita turned. There at the edge of the clearing stood Mrs. Zimmermann. The folds of her dress were filled with orange fire, and her homely wrinkled face was lit by the light of invisible footlights. A purple halo hovered about her, and its light fell upon the gray grass.

"Stop, Rose Rita! Stop what you're doing and listen to me!"

Rose Rita hesitated. She took the ring between her thumb and finger and started to take it off. It was on tight, but it could be moved. Now the voice in Rose Rita's head got louder. It told her not to listen to Mrs. Zimmermann. It told her that she had the right to be happy, to do what she wanted to do.

Rose Rita swallowed hard and licked her lips. She turned toward the shadow that waited, hovering, nearby. "I . . . I want to be a . . ."

Mrs. Zimmermann spoke again in a loud echoing com-

manding voice that seemed to fill the whole clearing. "I command you, Rose Rita, to give me that ring! Give it to me now!"

Rose Rita stood, hesitating. Her eyes were wide with fear. Then, like a sleepwalker, she turned and walked toward Mrs. Zimmermann. As she walked, she began working the ring loose from her finger. Up it slid, painfully, from one joint to the next. It was off now and lying in the palm of her right hand. Mrs. Zimmermann reached out and took it. She glanced at it scornfully and slipped it into the pocket of her dress. The halo faded and the footlights died. The folds of Mrs. Zimmermann's dress were just black creases now.

"Hi, Rose Rita," said Mrs. Zimmermann, smiling. "Long time no see."

Rose Rita looked nervously behind her, but the shadow was gone. Then she collapsed into Mrs. Zimmermann's arms and sobbed. Her whole body shook, and as she cried, she felt as if she were getting something poisonous and putrid out of her system. When she had cried herself out, Rose Rita stepped back and looked at Mrs. Zimmermann. Her face was pale and drawn, but her eyes were cheerful. She looked and talked like herself.

"What . . . what happened to you, Mrs. Zimmermann?" was all Rose Rita could think of to say.

Mrs. Zimmermann laughed softly. "I might ask you the same question, my dear. By the way, were you scared of me when I showed up just now?"

"I sure was. I was afraid you'd wave your wand and . . . hey!" Suddenly Rose Rita remembered. Mrs. Zimmermann's wand had been destroyed, and she had not made another. She was next-door to powerless as a witch. Then how . . . ?

Mrs. Zimmermann could tell what Rose Rita was thinking. She laughed again. It was a pleasant sound, and nothing like Gert Bigger's insane giggle. "Rose Rita," she said, chuckling, "you have been flimflammed. I bluffed you. You see, I can still make myself look pretty darned terrifying, with footlights and haloes and all, but if you had chosen to go on with what you were doing, I wouldn't have been able to do a thing to stop you. Not a blessed thing."

Rose Rita stared at the ground. "I'm glad you bluffed me, Mrs. Zimmermann. I almost did something awful. But . . . but what happened to you? The other night, I mean. Where did you come from just now?"

"From the chicken yard," said Mrs. Zimmermann, smiling wryly. "Haven't you guessed by now?"

Rose Rita's mouth dropped open. "You mean . . . you mean you were . . . ?"

Mrs. Zimmermann nodded. "Uh-huh. And I'll never be able to look a plate of chicken salad in the face again, as long as I live. Gertie did that to me with the ring. But in order for me to have been brought back to my proper shape, something must have happened to her. Do you know what it was?"

Rose Rita was utterly confused. "I . . . I thought maybe you had figured out some way to break the spell she put on you. Isn't that what you did?"

Mrs. Zimmermann shook her head. "No, my dear. Even in the days when I had my magic wand, I would not have been strong enough to defeat someone who had a ring like that one. No, Rose Rita. All I know is this: one minute I was behind that fence, leading my, uh . . ." (she coughed) ". . . my, uh, chickeny life, and the next minute, I was standing there like my old self. Something must have happened. Maybe you can tell me what."

Rose Rita scratched her head. "You got me, Mrs. Zimmermann. Mrs. Bigger was gonna kill me with a spell, but in the middle of it all, she disappeared. She was gonna use the ring to call on . . . to call on . . ." It was strange, but now that she didn't have the ring on her finger anymore, Rose Rita couldn't remember the name of the devil that Mrs. Bigger had called on.

"Asmodai?" said Mrs. Zimmermann.

"Gee. That's it. How'd you know?"

"I didn't get a doctorate in Magic Arts from the University of Göttingen for nothing. Go on."

"Well, she called on whatsisname, and she said she wanted to be young and beautiful and live for . . . for a thousand years, I think it was. Anyway, she disappeared, so I figure the magic must have worked. But I guess she didn't know there'd be an earthquake along with all the rest of the presto-chango. The coins slid off my eyes, and that's how I got loose."

"Lucky for you," said Mrs. Zimmermann. "I'm sure old Gertie didn't count on that happening. And there may have been some other things she wasn't counting on."

"Huh? What do you mean?"

"I'm not sure what I mean, just yet. Right now, however, I think we'd better be getting back to the store. When I ducked out of the chicken yard, there was an incredible ruckus going on inside the store. It sounded like they were turning the place inside out. But I figured you needed me more than they did. I just barely caught sight of you as you were hightailing it for the woods. I'm an old woman, and I can't run very fast, so you got ahead of me. But I didn't have any trouble following you. You left quite a trail in the underbrush. And anyway, I was a girl scout leader back in the old days. Come on."

As it was, Rose Rita and Mrs. Zimmermann didn't have much trouble finding their way back to the store. They followed the swath of trampled grass and broken branches and muddy footprints back to the little path, and from there on it was easy.

Later the two of them were trotting briskly along the needle-strewn path when all of a sudden Mrs. Zimmermann said, "Look!" She pointed off to the left, and there Rose Rita saw a young slender willow tree. It stood, all alone, amid tall pines.

"Look at what?" said Rose Rita, puzzled.

"That willow."

"Oh yeah. It's just a tree. What about it?"

"What about it? Well, for one thing, you don't usually see willows all by themselves in the middle of pine forests. You find them in willow groves, by the banks of rivers and lakes and streams. And there's something else wrong. Its leaves are trembling. Can you feel any wind?"

"Nope. Gee, that is weird. Do you think maybe it's blowing over there, but not here?"

Mrs. Zimmermann rubbed her chin. "Tell me, Rose Rita," she said suddenly. "Can you remember the exact words Mrs. Bigger used? When she got herself changed, I mean."

Rose Rita thought. "Gee, I don't think I can. Something about being young and beautiful and living a long time, like I said before."

"That tree is young, and it certainly is beautiful," said Mrs. Zimmermann quietly. "As for how long it will live, I really couldn't say."

Rose Rita looked at the tree, and then she looked at Mrs. Zimmermann. "You mean . . . you mean you think . . ."

"Like I said before, I don't know what I think. That is, I'm not sure. But something had to happen to return me to my present shape. If a witch is changed into something else—a tree, for instance—she isn't a witch any longer, and all her enchantments are broken. Come on, Rose Rita. Time's a-wasting. We'd better get back."

It was fully daylight when Rose Rita and Mrs. Zimmermann stepped out into the clearing behind Gert Bigger's store. They walked around to the front and found Aggie Sipes and her mother standing there. They were watching the two policemen, who, in turn, were staring at some things that lay piled on the front steps of the store. It was quite an odd collection. A funeral pall, a big wooden cross, some brown beeswax candles, a tarnished silver censer, a gilded incense boat, and an aspergillum—otherwise known as a holy water sprinkler. There was a big pile of books, too. Among them was the book that Rose Rita had found on Gert Bigger's bedside table.

As soon as Aggie caught sight of Rose Rita coming around the corner of the store, she gave a wild yell and ran toward her.

"Rose Rita, you're okay! Gee, I thought you were dead! Wow! Hooray! Whee!" Aggie hugged Rose Rita and jumped up and down. Mrs. Sipes came over too. There was a big smile on her face.

"Are you Mrs. Zimmermann?" she asked.

"I am," said Mrs. Zimmermann. The two women shook hands.

The two policemen walked over and joined the welcoming committee. They looked suspicious, as policemen often do. One of them had a note pad and a pencil in his hand.

"Okay," he said brusquely. "Are you the Mrs. Zigfield that got lost last night?"

"Yes. Zimmermann's the name, by the way. Please excuse my appearance, but I've been through quite a lot." Mrs. Zimmermann did indeed look as if she had spent the last two nights in the woods. Her dress was tattered and torn and had burrs all over it. Her shoes were wet and muddy, and her hair was a mess. There was pine pitch all over her hands and her face.

"Yeah," said Rose Rita. "We . . . we uh . . ." She realized with a sudden shock that she couldn't tell these people what had happened. Not and expect to be believed, that is.

"We, ah, had quite an experience, the two of us," Mrs. Zimmermann cut in quickly. "You see, I went walking out behind the Gunderson farm night before last, and I got lost in the woods. I know you'll think I was daffy for going out in the rain like that, but the fact is, I like walking in the rain. I love the sound of rain hitting the fabric of an umbrella—it's sort of a cozy sound, like rain on a tent roof. I hadn't intended to walk very far, but before I knew it, there I was, off the path and lost. Then, to make matters worse, the wind started blowing up a gale, and it blew my umbrella inside out, so I had to throw it away. Too bad too, because it was such a nice umbrella. But as I was saying, I got lost, and I've been wandering about for two days. Luckily I studied botany in college, and I know a little about what herbs and berries are safe to eat. So I'm a bit worn out, but otherwise okay, I think. Just by chance I ran into Rose Rita, and she guided me back to civilization. And from what she tells me, she's had quite a horrifying experience herself. It seems that the old lady who runs this store had her bound and gagged and locked in a closet. Then she gave her some drug and took her out into the woods and left her to starve. Fortunately Rose Rita knows a little wood-craft, and she was on her way back when she met me. Also," she added, reaching into her pocket, "we found this out in the woods, and when it got light, we were able to use it to help us find our way back."

It was Aggie's boy scout knife! The knife with the compass in the handle. Mrs. Zimmermann had found it where Aggie dropped it in Gert Bigger's back yard.

Rose Rita stared at Mrs. Zimmermann in pure admira-tion. She had told some good lies in the past, but never any quite as good as this one of Mrs. Zimmermann's. But then Rose Rita remembered Aggie. She knew the real story of how Mrs. Zimmermann had disappeared. And she knew about the knife, since she was the one who had dropped it. Would she spill the beans? Rose Rita glanced nervously at her and saw, to her surprise and irritation, that Aggie was trying hard to suppress a giggle. It was the first time Rose Rita had ever seen Aggie laugh.

But Aggie said nothing, and fortunately her mother did not notice the laughing fit that had come over her. The policeman with the note pad hadn't noticed either.

He had been busy jotting down every word Mrs. Zimmermann said. "Okay now," he said, looking up from his work. "Mrs. Zigfield, you got any idea what happened to the old lady that ran this store?"

Mrs. Zimmermann shook her head. "None whatsoever, officer. Can't you find her?"

"Nope. But we're gonna put out an all points bulletin for her arrest. Boy was she crazy! Did you see all this stuff?" He pointed toward the pile at the foot of the steps.

Mrs. Sipes looked at Mrs. Zimmermann with wide worried eyes. "Mrs. Zimmermann, what do you make of all this? Do you think Mrs. Bigger was a witch?"

Mrs. Zimmermann stared straight at her. "A *what?*"

"A witch. I mean, look at all these things. I can't imagine why else she would have . . ."

Mrs. Zimmermann put her tongue between her teeth and made a *tsk-tsk* sound. She shook her head slowly. "Mrs. Sipes," she said, in a shocked voice, "I don't know what you've been telling your daughter, but this is the twentieth century. There are no such things as witches."

CHAPTER THIRTEEN

When the Pottingers arrived at the Sipes farm later that morning, they found the Sipeses, their eight children, Mrs. Zimmermann, and Rose Rita, all huddled around a radio on the front porch of the farmhouse. They were listening to a radio report on what had come to be known as "the Petoskey witch case." The Pottingers were, of course, pretty tense to begin with, but when they found out that their daughter had, for a little while, been the prisoner of an elderly lunatic who imagined herself to be a witch—well, they really got the jitters. Mrs. Zimmermann did her best to calm them down. She pointed out that, after all, she and Rose Rita were safe, and the whole adventure—terrifying as it had been—was over. It seemed clear that if he could have found some way to do it, Mr. Pottinger would have blamed the whole affair on Mrs. Zimmermann's "screwballishness," but he didn't have time to do any blaming, what with all the fuss and flurry and tearful reunions going on around him. Mr. Sipes, who had come back from his business trip earlier that morning, took Mr. Pottinger out to show him the barn, and the Pottingers were invited to stay for lunch.

Around two that afternoon the Pottingers drove back to New Zebedee with Rose Rita. Rose Rita and Aggie had a tearful farewell at the car window, and they promised to write to each other a lot during the next year. The last thing that Aggie said as the Pottingers were about to drive away was, "I hope you don't get a flat tire. They're awful hard to fix." Mrs. Zimmermann stayed behind. She said, rather mysteriously, that she had some "business to attend to." Rose Rita figured that it had something to do with the magic ring, but she knew from past experience that Mrs. Zimmermann wouldn't tell her anything more until she was darned good and ready.

About a week after she got back to New Zebedee, Rose Rita received a purple-bordered letter in the mail. Inside was a piece of lavender-colored stationery, and on it this message was written:

My dear,

I'm back, and so is Lewis—for the time being. It seems that the pump that supplies the water to his camp broke down, and they're sending the kids home till they get it fixed. Sometime or other, Lewis will be going back for the rest of the camp session, but in the meantime, you are hereby invited to a coming-home-from-camp-for-now party for Lewis at my cottage on Lyon Lake next Saturday. Plan to stay overnight. If it's okay with your folks, I'll be around to get you in Bessie after lunch. It should be a lot of fun. Bring your swimming suit.

> *Yours,*
> *Florence Zimmermann*

PS: Don't bring any presents for Lewis. He's bringing home enough stuff from camp as it is.

Rose Rita had no trouble persuading her mother to let her spend the night at Mrs. Zimmermann's cottage. And so on Saturday off she went, valise in hand, to Lyon Lake. All the way out to the cottage Rose Rita tried to find out if Mrs. Zimmermann had discovered anything about the ring. But Mrs. Zimmermann said nothing. When they pulled into the driveway of the cottage, there was another car parked in front of them. Jonathan's car.

"Hi, Rose Rita! Gee, you look great!" There was Lewis. He was wearing his bathing suit.

"Hi, yourself," Rose Rita yelled, waving. "Where'd you get that sun tan? Out at the camp?"

Lewis grinned happily. He had been hoping she would notice. "Yeah. Hey, hurry up and get into your suit. Last one in is a wet hen!" Lewis reddened and covered his mouth with his hand. He had heard some of the story of Gert Bigger and the ring from Jonathan, and he knew what he had said.

Rose Rita glanced quickly at Mrs. Zimmermann, who was coughing rather loudly and trying to blow her nose at the same time.

As soon as Rose Rita had gotten her suit on, she ran down the long sloping lawn and dived into the water. Lewis was there ahead of her. He was swimming! Back and forth, up and down. It was only dog paddling, but for Lewis, that was something. For as long as Rose Rita had known him, Lewis had been scared of the water. Usually when he went in, he just stood around and splashed, or floated on an inner tube.

Rose Rita was overjoyed. She had always wanted for Lewis to know how to swim, so they could go swimming together. Of course, he was still scared of deep water, but he was getting more confident. Next year, he said, he'd get his Intermediate Swimmer's card for sure.

Later Rose Rita and Lewis were sitting on the lawn with towels wrapped around them. Nearby, on lawn chairs, were Jonathan and Mrs. Zimmermann. Jonathan was wearing his white linen suit, which he only wore on special occasions during the summer. The last special occasion had been V-J Day, so the suit was looking rather yellow, and it smelled of mothballs. Mrs. Zimmermann was wearing a new purple dress. She had thrown away the one she had been wearing on her vacation, because there were so many unpleasant memories associated with it. She looked rested and healthy. On a small table between her and Jonathan was a pitcher of lemonade and a plate heaped with chocolate chip cookies.

Lewis looked at Mrs. Zimmermann with awe. He was dying to ask her what it had felt like to be a chicken, but he couldn't think of any polite way of putting the question. Besides she was likely to be sensitive on the subject. So Lewis just ate his cookie and drank his lemonade and said nothing.

"All right, Florence," said Jonathan, puffing impatiently at his pipe. "We're all dying to know. What did you find out about the ring? Eh?"

Mrs. Zimmermann shrugged. "Almost nothing. I searched high and low in Oley's house, but all I found were these." She dug into a pocket of her dress and handed Jonathan three or four very rusty iron rings.

"What are these?" he said, turning them over. "Are they rejects from Oley's magic ring factory?"

Mrs. Zimmermann laughed. "No . . . at least, I don't think they are. I found them in a bowl in the back of the cupboard in Oley's kitchen. Do you really want to know what I think they are?"

"What?"

"Well, the Vikings used to wear leather breastplates with iron rings sewed to them. They called the breastplates byrnies, I think. Anyway, these rings look like some I saw once in a museum in Oslo. I think Oley must have dug these up, along with the arrowheads—and the ring."

"Now wait a minute, Florence. I know I've got a beard, but it's not long and white, and I've still got most of my marbles. Are you trying to tell us that the Vikings brought that ring over to America with them?"

"I'm not trying to tell you anything, Weird Beard. I'm just showing you what I found. You can think what you like. I'm just saying that these rings *look* like Viking artifacts. The Vikings roamed all over the world. They even went to Constantinople. And a lot of the treasure of the ancient world found its way there. There are a thousand other ways they might have found the ring, of course. I don't know. As I say, you can think what you darned please."

Mrs. Zimmermann and Jonathan got into a long pointless argument over whether or not the Vikings ever came to America. In the middle of all this, Lewis interrupted.

"Excuse me, Mrs. Zimmermann, but . . ."

Mrs. Zimmermann smiled at Lewis. "Yes, Lewis? What is it?"

"Well, I was just wondering . . . are you sure it really was King Solomon's ring?"

"No, I'm not sure," said Mrs. Zimmermann. "Let's just say that I think it's likely. After all, the ring behaved the way Solomon's ring was supposed to behave. So it probably was that very same ring. On the other hand, there are lots of stories about magic rings that are supposed to have really existed. Some of the stories are true, and some of them are false. It might have been one of the other rings, like the ring of the Nibelungs. Who knows? I am, however, fairly sure that it was magic."

"What did you do with the darned ring?" asked Jonathan.

"Hah! I've been waiting for you to ask that! All righty. If you must know, I melted it down in Oley's cookstove. One of the properties of gold is that it will melt at a fairly low temperature. And from all I know about magic, once a magic ring loses its original shape, it loses its powers too. Just to be on the safe side, however, I put the ring (or what was left of it) in a baby food jar along with some lead sinkers. Then I rented a rowboat and rowed out on Little Traverse Bay, and dropped the jar into the drink. Good riddance to bad rubbish, as my father used to say."

Lewis could not contain himself any longer. He had heard from Rose Rita the story of how Mrs. Zimmermann had failed to remake her magic umbrella, and he felt bad about it. He wanted Mrs. Zimmermann to be the greatest magician in the world. "Mrs. Zimmermann!" he burst out. "How come you wrecked the ring? You could've used it, couldn't you? I mean, it wasn't really evil, was it? You could've done something really good with it, I'll bet!"

Mrs. Zimmermann gave Lewis a sour look. "You know who you sound like, Lewis? You sound like those people who keep telling us that the atomic bomb is a really wonderful thing, that it isn't really evil, though it has been put to evil purposes." Mrs. Zimmermann heaved a deep sigh. "I suppose," she said slowly, "I *suppose* that Solomon's ring—assuming that that's what it really was—could have been put to some good use. I thought about that before I melted the thing down. But I said to myself, 'Do you really think you're such an angelic creature that you could resist the urge to do nasty things with that ring?' Then I asked myself, 'Do you want to sit on the blamed thing for the rest of your life, always worrying and fidgeting for fear someone like Gert Bigger might grab it away from you?' The answer to both those questions was no, and that is why I decided to get rid of the ring. As you may know, Lewis, I don't have much magic power anymore. And you know what? It's a relief! I'm going to spend the rest of my days snapping matches out of the air and trying to beat Weird Beard over here at poker. Not," she added, with a sly glance at Jonathan, "that either of those things takes a great deal of talent to do."

Jonathan stuck out his tongue at Mrs. Zimmerman and then both of them laughed. It was a happy relaxed sound, and Lewis and Rose Rita joined in.

There was more swimming, and more eating. After the sun went down, Jonathan built a bonfire down on the beach, and they all roasted marshmallows and sang songs. Lewis handed around presents. They were all things he had made at scout camp. He gave Jonathan a copper ash-tray, and he gave Mrs. Zimmermann a necklace of purply-white seashells. To Rose Rita he gave a leather belt and a neckerchief slide that he had whittled. It was painted green with yellow spots, and the lump on the front was supposed to look like a toad. Well, at any rate, it had eyes.

Much later that evening, after Lewis and Jonathan had gone home, Rose Rita and Mrs. Zimmermann were sitting by the embers of the bonfire. Out across the darkened lake they could see the lights of other cottages. From somewhere came the sleepy drone of a motorboat.

"Mrs. Zimmermann?" said Rose Rita.

"Yes, my dear? What is it?"

"There's a couple of things I have to ask you. First of all, how come that ring didn't put the old whammy on you the way it did on me when I picked it up? When I gave it to you, you just looked at it as if you couldn't have cared less, and then you stuck it in your pocket. How come?"

Mrs. Zimmermann sighed. Rose Rita heard her snap

her fingers, and she saw the brief tiny flare of a match, and she smelled cigar smoke. "Why wasn't I affected?" said Mrs. Zimmermann, as she puffed. "You know, that's a good question. I guess it's because I'm really happy the way I am. You see, I think a ring like that can only exercise power over someone who isn't satisfied with himself. Or herself."

Rose Rita blushed. She still felt ashamed of what she had tried to do with the ring. "Did . . . did you ever tell Uncle Jonathan what . . . what I was gonna do when you stopped me?"

"No," said Mrs. Zimmermann softly. "I did not. As far as he knows, the ring dragged you off to some mysterious meeting with the devil. Remember, you never actually said what you wanted to do, though it wasn't hard for me to guess. And by the way, don't feel so bad. Lots of people would have wished for worse things than you wished for. Far worse things."

Rose Rita was silent for a while. Finally she said, "Mrs. Zimmermann, do you think I'll have a lousy time in school this fall? And what about when I'm a grownup? Will things be different then?"

"My dear," said Mrs. Zimmermann slowly and deliberately, "I may be a witch, but I'm not a prophet. Seeing into the future was never my line, even when I had my magic umbrella. But I will tell you this: You have a lot of wonderful qualities. When you tried to drive Bessie, for example. Lots of girls your age would've been too chicken even to try. That took guts. It also took guts to break into Mrs. Bigger's store in the hope that you might be able to rescue me. And another thing: The women who are remembered in history, women like Joan of Arc and Molly Pitcher, are not remembered because they spent all their time powdering their noses. As for the rest, you'll just have to wait and see how your life turns out. That's all I can say."

Rose Rita said nothing. She poked in the ashes with a stick while Mrs. Zimmermann smoked. After a while, the two of them got up, kicked some sand over the fire, and went to bed.

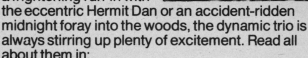

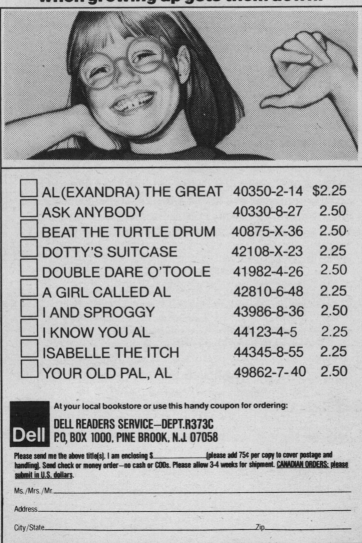

JudyBlume

knows about growing up. She has a knack for going right to the heart of even the most secret problems and feelings. You'll always find a friend in her books —like these, from YEARLING:

____ARE YOU THERE, GOD?
IT'S ME, MARGARET...........................$2.50 (40419-3)

____BLUBBER $2.50 (40707-9)

____FRECKLE JUICE $1.95 (42813-0)

____IGGIE'S HOUSE $2.50 (44062-9)

____THE ONE IN THE MIDDLE
IS THE GREEN KANGAROO...............$1.95 (46731-4)

____OTHERWISE KNOWN AS SHEILA
THE GREAT $2.50 (46701-2)

____SUPERFUDGE $2.50 (48433-2)

____TALES OF A FOURTH GRADE
NOTHING...$2.50 (48474-X)

____THEN AGAIN, MAYBE I WON'T $2.75 (48659-9)

YEARLING BOOKS